W9-BWQ-167

THE TIME HAS NOT YET COME

THE TIME HAS NOT YET COME

•

Michael Dearmin

AVALON BOOKS
NEW YORK

Published by Avalon Books,
an imprint of Thomas Bouregy & Co., Inc.
New York, NY

Library of Congress Cataloging-in-Publication Data

Dearmin, Michael.
    The time has not yet come / Michael Dearmin.
        p.   cm.
    ISBN 978-0-8034-7621-9 (hardcover : acid-free paper)
1. Murder—Investigation—Fiction.   I. Title.
    PS3604.E19T56 2011
    813'.6—dc23

                                            2011025794

PRINTED IN THE UNITED STATES OF AMERICA
ON ACID-FREE PAPER
BY RR DONNELLEY, HARRISONBURG, VIRGINIA

Dedicated to my amazing wife, Jennifer, without whose love, support, and encouragement this undertaking would not have been possible; to my children, Patricia, Michelle, John, and Michael; and especially to Uhura, the best birthday present a man could ever receive.

Acknowledgments

I want to express my thanks to all who offered criticism and advice in getting this initial work completed. A special thank-you to Dr. Harry Donaghy and to the late Dr. George Gross, both of whom took the time to read a draft of the novel and offer very constructive criticism. Thanks also to Twilamp, including Charline Palmtag for her numerous editorial suggestions, most of which I accepted, and Mara Skarry (pronounced "scary"—she isn't, but she thinks she is) for her tireless efforts on my behalf. She is a very special agent and a very special person. I must also thank Randall Platt, who encouraged me not to give up, and Elmer Kelton, whose work inspired me to attempt this venture. Thanks also to Geri Nelligan for putting up with her cantankerous little brother for lo these many years. Finally, I want to acknowledge Dr. William Taylor, who has provided such excellent care and attention to our many pets over the last several years, and most especially the extraordinary care he provided to our big girl, who was the model for Drella.

Chapter One

Out in front of the general store, Henry Johnson shook the storekeeper's hand. Johnson was a rancher who, with his daughter, Maria, had a small spread a couple of miles out of town. A stocky man with shiny black hair that lay in tight curls around his head, he had a kind face that had seen its share of trials, and his skin was a dark brown as a result of the many hours he had spent working in the sun. "I want to thank you, Paul. When that order comes in, I'll be able to store much more winter feed in my barn."

"Glad I could help, Henry," Paul Higgens said. Higgens was a slight man with a pallor indicative of his indoor business. His hair was thinning and mostly gray, and he was constantly pushing his ill-fitting glasses up the bridge of his nose. "By the way, how are you and John Culbertson getting along? Is he still trying to get you to sell out to him?"

"He's trying," Henry replied, "but I think he knows that there's no way Maria would let go of the ranch. Not with her mother buried there. Besides, the place is beginning to show a little profit. I told Culbertson the last time he brought the question up that even if I wanted to sell, Maria would never agree."

The storekeeper laughed. "That daughter of yours sure has a mind of her own," he said. "Well, I'll get that order off right away, Henry, and when it comes in, I'll send someone out to let you know. Shouldn't be more than five or six weeks."

"Thanks, Paul," Henry said, and he turned and started down the street. As he drew abreast of the sheriff's office, the door opened and sheriff Bob Gordon came out, followed by several Circle C riders.

"Why, hello, Henry," the sheriff said, clapping him on the shoulder. "I was just heading down to the Lucky Lady. Can I buy you a beer? The boys here were just talking about trying to get a game of cards going. I can't play because I have some business to attend to, but maybe you'd like to sit in for a few hands."

Henry Johnson knew that he had a weakness for poker, but that knowledge didn't mean that he would pass up a game if one came along. "Thank you, Sheriff. A beer and a friendly game of cards sounds like just the thing before I head back to the ranch. No time for games there."

They pushed through the batwing doors, stopped at the bar for drinks, and moved to a table. Several hours passed, and Henry lost many more hands than he won. The saloon was nearly empty, and Henry pushed his chair back and got up. "That does it for me. My daughter's going to have my hide for being so late, especially when she finds out how much I lost tonight. Thanks, boys. I'll see you later."

The remaining men at the table nodded and watched Henry move through the door. Then the three rose as one and followed him out.

Chapter Two

Matthew Stoker stepped down from the Appaloosa and surveyed the valley below. He was just over six feet tall, ruggedly handsome, and graying at the temples. His attire was tasteful. The Colt on his hip belonged there as much as the hat on his head. Matt rolled himself a smoke, lit it, and gazed out over the valley. His dog, a large black shorthair, lay down beside him and watched the squirrels scurrying around the nearby fir trees. Matt took particular note of the ranch house off in the distance.

"You know, Drella," Matt said, talking to the dog, a habit he had gotten into shortly after he found her, "I bet we can get a drink of good, cold well water at that ranch down there." The dog turned her head and looked at him for a second, and then turned back to watch a squirrel busying itself among the pinecones.

"We should get there about noon time," Matt continued. "If we're lucky, we might get a little dinner too. What do you think of that?" Drella's tail thumped the ground when she heard the word *dinner,* but she kept her attention on the squirrel. Matt finished his smoke and then swung back up into his saddle. He reined the Appaloosa, Aphrodite, around and set out toward the ranch on the other side of the valley. The dog took one last look at the squirrel and then trotted after Matt and Aphrodite.

Maria Johnson set the pies on the windowsill to cool. As she did, she caught a glimpse of sunlight from something metal way up in the pass. *Someone is coming into the valley,* she thought to herself, and went on about her business. She was an attractive woman in her early twenties. She did not have the type of beauty that made men fall all over themselves when they met her. Rather, she was almost regal in her bearing. Her long auburn hair, high cheekbones, and lithe body radiated an inner beauty, while her flashing green eyes suggested a feisty quality that one would do well to avoid encountering. She and her father were trying to work their small spread by themselves with the help of an occasional hired hand during the busiest times. She picked up a bucket and went out to the barn, fed the livestock, and did the milking. As she was going back to the house, she saw a rider far off in the distance. *He'll probably turn off north toward the Culbertson Ranch,* she thought as she entered the house. She was a little concerned about her father. He'd gone to town the day before and should have been back by now. He probably stayed late, enjoying his time away from the daily trials of keeping their heads above water. Maria wasn't upset. Her father was a good man who worked hard. He deserved a little fling once in a while.

Maria had finished her household chores and sat down

at the table with a cup of coffee. She looked out the window again and saw that the rider had passed the cutoff to the Culbertson Ranch. Now she wished her father were here. It was a worry to be alone with a stranger riding in. She got up and took the Winchester from the rack on the wall, levered a cartridge into the chamber, and stood it on its stock by the front door. Then she returned to the table and her coffee. If the rider was heading for her place, he was still about an hour and a half away, at the pace he was moving. She sipped her coffee and watched his approach.

Matt rode up into the front yard. "Sit, girl!" Drella sat immediately. "Hello, is anyone home?"

Picking up the rifle by the door, Maria moved to the front window. She immediately realized that this man was not a ranch hand. He wore black store-bought pants and coat, his gloves weren't worn working gloves, and his boots had no spurs attached. It was apparent that the handgun, holster, and gun belt around his waist were more than accessories. His hat, while somewhat dusty, showed no signs of wear and tear, and his boots were polished and unscuffed. He did not instill in Maria a sense of fear or concern, but she judged him as a man who was not to be taken lightly. She pushed the window open, making sure her rifle was in view.

"What can I do for you?" she asked.

"I sure would appreciate a chance at the pump for myself and my animals," Matt said.

"Help yourself," she said. "You're welcome to as much as you'd like."

Matt stepped down from his horse and walked to the pump. He filled the bucket and held it out for his horse to drink. Then he put more water in the bucket and offered it to the dog. While the dog drank, Matt brushed the dust from his pants and hat. Then he took off his coat, shook it several times, and brushed the remaining dust from its surface. Only when the dog had finished drinking did he empty the bucket and get some water for himself.

Maria, who had been watching from the window, was impressed by his concern for his animals and the meticulous attention he paid to them, as well as to himself. Setting the Winchester down, she called out to him. "Would you like something to eat?"

"That's awfully kind of you, ma'am," he said. "I could stand some cooking that's not my own."

Maria disappeared from the window. Matt turned and loosened the cinch on his horse. Then he moved to the woodpile by the side of the house. "Might as well try to pay for our dinner, huh, Drella?"

He picked up the ax and started chopping. After a few minutes, he had produced a considerable pile of kindling. He then turned, walked back to the pump, and washed his face and hands with the cold well water.

Maria came out of the house carrying two plates. Matt noted that she was really quite attractive. She was young and not yet worn down by the demands of life in a harsh land. Her beauty was the type that reflected a woman of strength and character.

"Just some leftover stew from last night," she said. "I thought your dog might like a plate too." She handed both plates to Matt. "Thanks for the kindling, but it wasn't necessary. May I pet your dog?"

"Sure. Just be careful." Maria hesitated. Matt laughed and said, "Don't worry. She won't bite the hand that feeds her. I just meant that you could end up with a friend for life." Maria smiled and knelt down beside the dog to scratch her behind her ear. "As for the kindling, you're welcome. It seemed like the least I could do. A lot of folks wouldn't be so quick to offer hospitality to a stranger," he said, watching her as she stroked Drella. "Would you like to feed her?" Maria nodded, and Matt handed one of the plates back to her. "Just tell her to sit and stay, put the plate down, and move away. Then, when you're ready, tell her 'okay.' "

"What's her name?" Maria asked.

"Oh, I'm sorry. Her name is Drella."

Maria turned toward the dog. "Drella, sit. Stay." The dog, who was focused on the plate, immediately sat down. Maria put the plate down and stepped back. The dog waited anxiously. "Okay, Drella." The dog, tail wagging, moved to the plate and began to eat.

"She doesn't gobble her food like other dogs, does she?"

Matt smiled and said, "No, she has always been a perfect lady."

"Drella, that's an unusual name."

"It's short for Cinderella." Matt smiled. "When I first found her, she was lying by the bushes, and she looked like a pile of ashes."

The dog finished the plate of stew and moved to Maria's side to nuzzle her hand in gratitude.

"You're welcome, Drella," she said.

"I know that it's none of my business, but do you live out here alone?" Matt asked.

"No, my father lives here as well," Maria replied, turning her eyes to the south toward town. "He went to town yesterday and hasn't returned yet. I'm beginning to get a little worried."

"Well, I need to get some supplies," Matt said, finishing the last bite of stew on his plate. "Show me the direction toward town, and I'll hunt him up and tell him you're concerned. What's his name?"

"Henry Johnson. I'm Maria Johnson," she said and then pointed. "Twin Forks is just over the hill about two miles."

"Matthew Stoker," Matt said, extending his hand. "Drella and I sure thank you for the stew."

After shaking hands, Matt turned and went to his horse, tightened the cinch, and swung effortlessly into the saddle. "I'll get word to your father," he said. "And thanks again for the meal; it was delicious. Let's go, big girl."

The dog, who had been lying beside Maria, got up and trotted over. Matt tipped his hat, turned, and headed in the direction Maria had indicated. After he had ridden out of earshot, he said, "Mighty pretty woman, don't you think, Drella? Must be terribly lonely out here with just her father. Probably has a lot of gentlemen callers, though. You sure took a shine to her."

The dog cocked her head and looked up at him. "Don't give me that look. I saw you making a fuss over her."

Chapter Three

Matt stopped at the tree line and looked back. Maria had left the yard and gone into the house. Then he caught sight of several riders coming from the north and heading for the Johnson spread. "What do you suppose that's about, hey, big girl?" The dog made no response, but the hair on her back was upright.

Maria saw the riders at nearly the same time. She figured it would be John Culbertson and wished her father were home. Not that she was afraid, but she knew the upcoming visit wouldn't be pleasant, and she would rather not be alone. When Culbertson and the other riders rode into the yard, she opened the door and stepped out on the porch.

Culbertson was a big man with a full beard, and one could see that the face beneath was weathered by time and nature. He had come to the valley about ten years before with a small herd of mavericks and had filed on as much land as he was allowed at the time. However, John Culbertson believed that all of the open range was rightfully his, and when others had come into the valley, they had been systematically driven off. Most believed Culbertson to be responsible. He had made several offers for the Johnson spread, but Henry and Maria had always turned him down.

The three riders with Culbertson showed the wear and tear common to ranch hands. They all wore Colts in holsters with leather thongs to tie them down when the men were not in the saddle. The four men swung their horses into a line in front of Maria. Culbertson touched the brim of his hat.

"Good afternoon, Maria."

"Mr. Culbertson."

"Your father about?"

"No, he isn't," Maria replied. "He went into town. I expect him back anytime now."

"Well, I don't wonder he hasn't come home yet," Culbertson said as he fished into his inside coat pocket and pulled out an official-looking document. "I hate to break the news to you, Maria, but your daddy lost his ranch to my foreman in a poker game last night, and Curly turned it over to me. Here's the deed with his signature on it."

For a moment she was taken by surprise. She knew that her father tended to lose money when he had been drinking. He always saw himself as a shrewd poker player, but, truth be known, he wasn't even as good as Maria. But surely he wouldn't think he could bet the ranch. Actually, she knew that he couldn't, but she would have to have a serious talk with him when he got home.

Maria turned her attention back to John Culbertson.

"I'm really very sorry, Mr. Culbertson, but I'm afraid my father has tried to take advantage of you. The deed to the ranch is in my name, not his."

Maria almost laughed when she saw the look on Culbertson's face. He had been so smug when he had ridden in. Now, he was confused as to what to do next. He looked around at his men, and then stammered, "B-b-but he's got to honor his gambling debts. You've got to honor his debts! It's the law."

"That may be, Mr. Culbertson," Maria replied, "but all of that would be between my father, you, and the law."

Culbertson's confusion changed to anger. "I have the deed to this property signed by your father. This ranch is mine!"

"If the lady's signature isn't on it, I don't think so."

Everyone turned and looked at Matt, who was leaning against the corner of the house, Drella sitting beside him. "She said the deed was filed in her name."

"Who the hell are you?" Culbertson asked.

"A friend of Miss Johnson's," Matt replied.

The rider closest to Matt began to edge his horse in such a manner as to take him out of Matt's sight. A low rumble came from Drella. "Easy, girl," Matt said quietly, keeping his attention on the other three men. "If that man of yours makes a move toward his Colt, my dog will let me know, and you for certain, Mr. Culbertson, and most probably he, will be dead."

"Are you threatening me?" Culbertson asked.

Matt straightened up and stepped away from the house, his right hand hanging by his side. "No, sir, Mr. Culbertson.

I never make threats," Matt said. "I simply want you and your man to understand that just because I can't see him doesn't mean he isn't being watched or that I don't know what he's doing. No threat, just an observation of the situation."

"Bart, get back over here," Culbertson growled. "We ain't looking for trouble, mister. What did you say your name was?"

"I didn't, but it's Matthew Stoker."

One of the riders leaned in and whispered something to Culbertson, who nodded and asked, "What brings you to these parts, gunfighter?"

"I can think of no reason why my business should be of any concern to you" was Matt's reply.

Culbertson, taken aback by this response, turned to Maria. "This isn't over. I'm going into town and talk to the sheriff. This place is going to be mine."

"Do what you have to do, Mr. Culbertson, but the sheriff can't change whose name is on the deed," Maria replied. "And I plan on living here and working this ranch for a long time. I'm not the least bit interested in selling to the Circle C or anyone else."

Culbertson reined his horse over near Matt. "Watch yourself, gunfighter. It might not be healthy to mix in the affairs of others."

Matt smiled. "Sound advice, Mr. Culbertson. I hope you heed it."

Culbertson turned his horse and rode out, the others falling in behind. Matt and Maria watched them ride off. When the group reached the road, three of the men headed toward town, while the other one rode off in the opposite direction. Matt's attention was focused on the single rider. "I wonder what that's all about," he murmured to himself. Drella looked at him quizzically, and then she got up and moved to the porch where Maria was standing.

"Well, Drella, do you always come to the assistance of maidens in distress?" Maria asked, lightly stroking the dog's head.

Matt, whose attention was still on the area where the single rider had disappeared, answered, "Yes, she does. I think it's because she was one once. She feels it's her duty."

"Drella was a maiden in distress?" Maria asked.

"It was a little more than three years ago when we met," Matt said. "I had made evening camp and just dished up a supper of stew and biscuits. As I sat down to eat, I heard a rustling in the nearby brush. After a few minutes, this dog crept out, crawling on her stomach. She was covered with dirt, and I could see her ribs. I held out a biscuit and called to her, but she wouldn't come, so I tossed the biscuit toward her. She shied away and then slowly crept toward the biscuit, sniffed it, and ate it. I then filled a plate with stew and moved toward her with the plate extended. She moved back into the brush, so I returned to my campfire, placed the plate on the ground with some biscuits alongside, and returned to my own meal. After several minutes, she slowly moved forward. When she was a couple of feet from the food, she darted in, grabbed a biscuit, and returned to her place to eat it. A few minutes later, the routine was repeated. Then she came back to nibble at the stew a few times. I watched for a while and then refilled the plate and crawled into my blankets. Several hours later, I awoke when I felt a weight on my leg. I looked down to find the dog lying beside me with her head on my leg. I glanced over and saw that the plate was empty. In the morning when I got up, she moved a few feet off, but she didn't show any sign of fear or aggression. We spent the next few days getting acquainted. I could see that she was just a puppy and had been mistreated. I brushed the dirt from her coat and treated the welts I discovered on her body. I named her Cinderella. Three days later, I judged her ready to travel. We have been the best of friends ever since."

Maria knelt down beside Drella, saying, "You poor thing. How could anyone have treated you so badly?"

Drella laid her head across Maria's knee and looked up at her affectionately, her tail thumping on the porch.

Matt moved to where he had left his horse. He gave her a pat on the neck and led her around to the front of the house. "I better head into town and see if I can locate your father. Do you have a gun?"

"Yes, I have a Winchester, and I know how to use it."

"Good, keep an eye on that group of trees off to the east when I ride out. If that waddy who's in there watching us starts heading toward you, get your rifle and stop him before he gets into the front yard."

Maria, who had not been aware that the rider had not appeared on the other side of the small grove of trees, asked, "You don't think he'll cause any trouble, do you?"

"No, ma'am. I think he's there to keep an eye on me, but just in case he doesn't follow me when I leave, I want you to be prepared to deal with him. I'm going to leave Drella here with you, and I'll pick her up when I come back with your father. Keep your eye on her; she'll let you know if anything is going on."

Matt moved to the dog and scratched her behind the ear. "You stay here and look after Maria, Drella. I'll be back soon. You be a good girl."

Matt swung up into the saddle, tipped his hat to Maria, told Drella to stay and guard, and started out. Drella whimpered softly but stayed where she was. Matt looked back. "It's okay, girl. I'll be back soon."

Maria and Drella watched Matt ride off and turn toward town. A few moments later, they watched Culbertson's hand ride out from the trees and follow Matt. When he was out of sight, Maria moved inside the house. Drella remained on the porch, looking in the direction that Matt had gone. Maria called to her, but the dog didn't move. "It's okay, Drella," Maria said as she moved back to where the dog was sitting. "He's not leaving you. He'll be back soon."

Chapter Four

Matt quickly became aware that the rider was following him. He also noticed that the man was keeping his distance, so he didn't worry much that he had a shadow. As he reached the top of a little hill, he saw the small town of Twin Forks about a mile ahead. The road he had been following branched just before the town. To the left a road moved down to a small stream and ran parallel to it. The right branch moved toward the foothills to the north. The main street of the town was built up around the center of the fork and then connected again with the other two roads at the opposite end of town. Matt reined in Aphrodite and moved off the road into a shallow wash that was surrounded by tall brush. He reached down and stroked the horse's neck.

"You know, Aphrodite, I think we'll just sit right here until that jasper that's following us rides on by. As a matter of fact, I think we'll just wait here until later in the afternoon."

Matt dismounted and loosened the cinch on the saddle.

17

Soon he heard the sound of a horse coming along the trail. The rider passed by and continued on toward town. It was the man that Culbertson had called Bart, and Matt was surprised that the rider paid no attention to the fact that Matt was no longer ahead of him. He watched the rider all the way into town and saw him tie his horse to the hitch rail and enter a two-story building that Matt assumed was a saloon. He guessed that the second story consisted of rooms that housed some of the employees, as well as providing an opportunity for a drover with a month's wages in his pocket to partake of additional services offered by the establishment.

Matt studied the rest of the town. At the end nearest him, across from the saloon that the rider had entered, there was a stable and blacksmith shop. There was a two-story building in the center of town that he guessed was a hotel or boardinghouse and several other buildings along both sides of the single main street. *Probably a general store, another saloon or two, certainly a sheriff's office, and maybe a restaurant,* Matt thought. At the far end were several small buildings, some with flowers. He guessed that these were the residences of those who ran businesses in the town. On the south side, there was a second street with only two buildings. One had a cross on top. The other was set back from the road and some distance away from the church. Matt guessed that building was probably a school or meetinghouse of some type. Matt looked around for a comfortable place to sit, reached inside his vest for the makings of a smoke, rolled one, and sat down to watch the town.

As the afternoon lengthened, he tightened the cinch, swung himself aboard Aphrodite, and headed toward town. He didn't ride straight in, but rather circled and came in alongside the livery stable. He dismounted and went inside, but there was no one around. Matt unsaddled the Appaloosa, put her in the first stall, found a sack of grain, and put a heaping scoop into the feeding trough. Then he took a brush down from the wall and began to brush the trail dust from Aphrodite.

"I'll take care of that, mister."

Matt turned around and saw a black man. He was about six foot one or two, two hundred pounds or so, and he looked as if he could take care of himself. "There wasn't anyone here when I came in," Matt said, "so I just went ahead and did for myself. How much do I owe you?"

"It's a dollar a day with grain extra, but insomuch as you've done everything yourself, I guess a dollar's enough. My name is Clay, Clay Harper." He offered his hand, and Matt shook it.

"Matthew Stoker," he said, noting that the grip was firm but did not offer the challenge that one frequently encountered in a first meeting. "Tell me, Clay, do you have a lawman around here? I'm looking for a man named Johnson and thought the law might know his whereabouts."

"The sheriff's office is across the street from the boardinghouse in the center of town, but if you're looking for Sheriff Gordon, you're more likely to find him in the Lucky Lady," Clay said. "I don't know if he'll be any help, though. I haven't seen Mr. Johnson around since late last night. He came in here, and I got him his horse. He said he was going to go down by the creek and get some sleep before heading home."

"Well, I just came from his place," Matt said. "His daughter is worried about him because he hasn't come home yet. Do you own this livery stable, Clay?"

"No, sir, I just work here. None of the ranches around here are hiring full-time help, and this is the only kind of work I can get here in town."

"Do you think you can show me the area along the creek where Johnson might have gone?" Matt asked. "I'll pay you for your time."

"Sure, and there's no need for you to pay me, Mr. Stoker. I like Mr. Johnson and Miss Maria. I've worked for them a couple of times when they've needed extra help. I've got a few things to take care of around here first, though. Take me about an hour," Clay said.

"Okay. Why don't I meet you at that saloon across the street in about an hour? And, Clay, it's Matthew."

Clay smiled. "All right, I'll see you in about an hour, Matthew."

Matt wandered around the town. It was pretty much as he had imagined it to be, and he was struck more by what it didn't have than what it did. There was no courthouse, no newspaper, no bank. The two-story building was a boardinghouse, rather than a hotel, and next to it was a county assay and land office. There was a café, but no fashionable dining establishment. It was a town that was just beginning to grow. The last shop in the business section, a barbershop and bathhouse, had obviously been built recently. The wood did not show much effect from the weather, and the paint still looked new. Matt entered the café and ordered a cup of coffee and a piece of apple pie. The place was empty because it was between mealtimes, but he was served quickly and courteously by the woman who ran the eatery.

"You new in town?" she asked.

"Just passing through. Have you been in business long?"

The woman reached under the counter and got a cup, poured coffee into it, and came over and sat down at Matt's table. She was a large, robust woman, but she moved in a graceful fashion. She was attractive in a noble yet matronly way.

"My husband and I came here a little more than two years ago. Before that we had a place across the river from Saint Jo. All day long we watched the people driving their wagons west. Business was good, but watching those people all day long finally wore off on us. So Jubal—that's my husband, Jubal Gaston—Jubal said, 'There must be something mighty nice out there if all these people are heading west. Why don't we pack up and see what's so almighty great that so many folks want to go there.' Well, you could have knocked me over with a feather! We were doing real fine with our restaurant right where we were, but once Jubal gets ahold of an idea, he doesn't let go of it very easy. So, we sold the place, packed up a wagon, and hooked on with a train heading west. When we saw this country, Jubal fell in love and decided that this was where we were going to start up again. My name is Constance, by the way, but most folks call me Ma because that's what Jubal is always calling me."

"Matthew Stoker. It's a pleasure to meet you."

"Lord, it's nice to run into a gent with manners. I don't see much of that around here except when the judge comes to town."

Matt smiled. "How is business? The town seems kind of small."

"It's small but getting bigger nearly every day. We do all right, especially on Saturdays when the hired hands come into town."

She told him that Twin Forks was currently negotiating with a doctor to get him to set up a practice locally. She also talked about the need for a newspaper and that the town was trying to attract an editor by offering to supply the building for the paper at cost. Matt was impressed with the enthusiasm of the woman and was convinced that Twin Forks was a town on the rise.

When Matt left the café, he headed across the street toward the Lucky Lady Saloon. He chuckled to himself, wondering how many Lucky Lady Saloons he had encountered in his travels. He figured there wasn't much imagination on the part of many saloon owners. He pushed through the batwing doors and took a look around. There were a couple of ranch hands at the bar, four more men playing cards at a table, and Culbertson and another man having a drink at still another table. The two men at the bar had been with Culbertson at the Johnson Ranch. The usual painting of a nearly nude woman lying on a chaise longue hung over the bar. Matt wondered how many knew that it was an imitation of Titian's *Venus of Urbino*.

A couple of saloon girls were standing at the end of the

bar, waiting for a lonely trail hand to buy them a drink in order to share in their company. One of the women took an interest in Matt as he moved to the bar, but he shook his head, and she stopped. Matt went to a corner of the bar where he could keep most of the room under surveillance and ordered a beer. The bartender drew him a mug of beer and placed it in front of him.

"You new in town?" the bartender asked.

Matt nodded his head. "Just passing through."

"Well, the first drink is on the house for newcomers, but everything else is cash only."

"Sounds reasonable."

One of the hands at the bar looked at Matt and said, "Hey, Hank, why don't you give him a real drink? How 'bout it, partner? Have a drink of whiskey on me."

"No, thanks."

"What's the matter, gunslinger? You too good to drink with the likes of me?"

Matt looked at the man who had turned to face him. He was young, in his midtwenties, of medium height, with blond hair and blue eyes. Matt was pretty certain that he wasn't a gunman, but he also knew that any fool with a gun could be dangerous, especially if he had been drinking, as this ranch hand obviously had.

"Mister, all I want to do is peaceably drink my beer," Matt said.

"The gunslinger thinks he's too good to drink with us, Pete."

"Come on, Billy. Let it alone," Pete said.

Billy stepped away from the bar, dropped his hands to

his sides, and said, "Let's see just how good you are, mister."

Matt shifted his beer to his left hand, took a sip from it, and said to the bartender, "Sure tastes good on a hot day."

"I said, let's see how good you are, gunfighter."

Matt straightened up from the bar and turned to face the hand they called Billy. "Look, son, I don't want to kill you, and you don't want to be dead." He continued to look at the man in front of him, but he said to Culbertson, "You're about to lose one of your hands, Mr. Culbertson, if you don't get him to back off."

Culbertson didn't move from the table, but he said, "Billy, give it a rest."

"This son of a bitch thinks he's too good to drink with me, and I don't take that from no one. Go on, gunslinger, make your play."

Matt kept his eyes on Billy, while at the same time taking in the rest of the room. Culbertson had pushed his chair back from the table. The card players had all stopped what they were doing and were watching the scene at the bar. Billy's friend had stepped out of the line of fire, and the bartender had pushed himself against the back wall. Billy's eyes indicated that he was getting anxious, and his hands were beginning to tremble. Matt just stood there, looking at him. Finally, Billy's hands started for his gun, but before it was halfway out of the holster, Matt's Colt was pointing at Billy's chest. Billy froze for a few seconds and then released the handle and let his gun drop back into the leather. Matt stepped forward and removed Billy's gun, turned and went back to his beer, and set the gun on the bar beside him. He took a large swallow, turned again to look at Billy, and said, "You're really not very fast at all, are you?" The bartender chuckled and the card players smiled, but no one laughed outright.

The man sitting with Culbertson stood up and tried to pull his gun belt up over his generous stomach. He failed. Matt watched him through the bar mirror as he strolled toward the end of the bar where Matt was standing.

"I'll take that," he said, gesturing toward the pistol Matt had placed on the bar.

Matt turned toward him and asked, "You his keeper?"

"I'm Sheriff Gordon," he said, pulling his coat open to reveal a badge pinned to his vest.

"And you just sat there through the entire thing?"

"I was waiting for someone to break the law. Couldn't do much till that happened, could I?" the sheriff said, grinning like an overweight Cheshire cat.

Matt studied him carefully. He had seen many men with a badge like Gordon, men who were not interested in the law but who were put in office to serve their own needs or those of someone with power. Gordon undoubtedly worked for Culbertson. If Billy had somehow managed to outdraw Matt and kill him, the sheriff would have called it self-defense; if Matt had gunned down Billy, he would be languishing in a cell waiting to be tried for murder. Under the present circumstances, there was little the sheriff could do, but Matt knew it would not be long before he was accused of breaking some law or another. Matt pushed Billy's Colt toward Gordon, who picked it up and stuck it in his belt. As he did so, Matt saw Clay standing just inside the swinging doors.

"Hey, Clay, buy you a beer?" Matt asked.

Gordon snorted and said, "You always buy drinks for useless no-accounts?"

Matt narrowed his eyes and stared at the lawman. "No. I didn't offer to buy you one," he said coldly.

Gordon stepped back as if he had been slapped in the face. His hand brushed his coat back and dangled near his Colt.

"You calling me a useless no-account?"

Matt smiled and said, "A rose by any other name . . ."

"What the hell does that mean?" Gordon sputtered. "I asked you, are you calling me a useless no-account?"

"Sheriff, all I did was answer your question in an appropriate manner. What you think it meant is entirely up to you. Now, why don't you just let it pass? If you're dead, you won't have the opportunity to arrest me for some crime that you haven't thought up yet."

Gordon, remembering what he had seen when Billy tried to outdraw the gunfighter, said, "You've made a big mistake, mister. Believe me, you don't want me for an enemy."

Matt chuckled, shook his head, and said, "I don't want you for anything at all."

Culbertson came over to the bar, took the sheriff by the arm, and led him back toward the table where they had been sitting.

"Come on, Bob. Let it go for now."

The sheriff continued to grumble but was not unwilling

to be led away. Matt turned toward Clay and asked, "How about that beer? Bartender."

Clay smiled and said, "I'm not allowed to have a drink in here."

"Really," Matt said. He turned to the bartender. "Is that right?"

"Yes, sir. It's Sheriff Gordon's orders. He owns this place."

Matt looked at Clay and said, "Why don't you go across and get saddled up? I'll just be a minute, and then we can get on about that business we talked about earlier."

Clay headed for the door, and Matt nodded to the bartender. "Why don't you bring me a couple of beers?"

The bartender moved to the keg, drew two schooners, and then brought them back and set them down in front of Matt.

"How much?" Matt asked.

"A nickel each. That'll make it ten cents."

"And how much for the glasses?" Matt asked.

"The glasses?" the bartender asked in surprise. Then a smile crossed his face and he nodded in understanding. "The glasses are ten cents each. That makes a total of thirty cents."

Matt tossed a silver dollar on the bar, picked up the beers, and started for the door. "Keep the change," he said with a smile and headed for the livery stable.

Chapter Five

Matt and Clay sat on a bale of hay, sipping their beers. Clay chuckled when Matt told him how he got the beers.

"Sure tastes good after a long day's work," Clay said. "I surely thank you. But don't underestimate Sheriff Gordon. He runs this town with an iron hand and not always legally, either."

"Don't worry about it. I seldom underestimate any man, particularly if he's a lawman. Still, any man should be able to have a drink when he feels the need." Then Matt asked, "Why do you stay around here when people treat you like that? Hell, I fought in a war that was supposed to do away with slavery and make men and women like you free."

"There are worse places. At least here, people mostly leave me alone," Clay said and then paused for a moment, thinking. "You know, I was lucky when I was a slave. My mother knew how to read and write and was the nanny and teacher to the master's children. As she taught them, she also taught me, and the master let me read the books he had in his library. I read a lot of literature and philosophy, and it taught me a great deal about people. So even though most folks don't understand me, I understand them. As a result, I'm able to navigate the waters of their fear and hatred."

Matt considered what Clay had said for a few moments; then he smiled and nodded. He got up and moved to Aphrodite's stall and slipped her hackamore over her head. "Why don't we head on down to that creek you mentioned and see if we can get a line on Mr. Johnson. Given what I've seen in this country, I have a feeling that something's rotten in the state of Denmark."

"You know Shakespeare?" Clay asked as he gathered his gear and bridled and saddled his horse.

"Some," Matt replied. "He can certainly turn a phrase. Sometimes I feel as if he can see into my soul. The man certainly understood human nature."

They both swung up on their mounts, and Clay led the way out of town.

Back at the saloon, Culbertson watched them ride out. He turned to the men playing cards at the table. "Ed, ride out and keep an eye on what's happening at the Johnson place. Pick up a bottle from the bar and some food from the kitchen. It may be a while before you're relieved. I want you to note all the comings and goings. Don't overdo on the bottle. I want you alert."

"Yes, sir, Mr. Culbertson," said one of the card players as he got up and headed for the bar.

Chapter Six

Matt and Clay reined up on a little knoll that overlooked a small creek. There were a few campsites along the edge of the stream where people who were just traveling through were beginning to set up for their evening meal. The two men rode down and asked several of the families that were camping on the banks if they had seen anything of a single man who might have been staying in the area. Everyone was friendly enough and some even invited Matt and Clay to stay for supper, but none had seen a lone rider.

One of the families had stopped the day before and decided to rest their team for an additional day. In answer to the questions put forth by Matt and Clay, they said that they had seen no one come down to the stream from the direction of town. They did mention that they had heard a gunshot early in the morning but never saw anyone. Matt asked from which direction the shot had come, and an older woman pointed to a wooded region just to the north of the little knoll where he and Clay had first come upon the creek.

"I had just come down to the water to fill the pot for morning coffee when I heard it. I thought maybe one of the other folks here might have stirred up a rabbit, but no one came out of the area to any of the camps. So, I guessed it must've been someone from the town out looking for breakfast," she said. She turned back to the pot on the fire, stirred it some, and said, "I got some good venison stew here, and you're both welcome to a plate."

Matt thanked her for the offer but declined, saying that they had better keep looking for their friend. The two rode off in the direction the woman had indicated. As they got into the wooded area, they started looking for tracks. The sun was beginning to sink behind the western hills, and the trees and brush made for tough going. Finally they came upon a narrow trail that seemed to lead in the direction of town. It was barely wide enough for the two to ride side by side.

"We might as well head back. It's going to get too dark to see anything pretty soon," Matt said.

Clay reined in and stared off to the left. "Have you ever seen brush grow like that?" he asked.

Matt followed Clay's gaze. He could see that a pile of brush had been propped up to appear as if it were growing. He guided Aphrodite over near the pile and dismounted. He pulled a part of the brush aside, revealing the body of a man lying facedown. Matt reached down and turned the man over on his back.

Clay, still on his horse, looked down at the body. "Well, you found Henry Johnson."

Matt looked around the area, but everything had been brushed clean. The only tracks were those left by Clay and him. He knelt down by Johnson and went through his pockets, finding only the makings and paper in his shirt pocket and a rabbit's foot in his pants. He tossed the rabbit's foot to Clay.

"Didn't do him much good, did it? Well, I think we'd better get the law down here," Matt said and added, "My guess is that Sheriff Gordon is going to try to use this to lock me up."

"Tell you what, Matt," Clay said. "I'll go in and see if I can find Earl Burns, Gordon's deputy. He's young, but I believe he's honest. And I also hear he's sweet on Johnson's daughter. You stay here until I get back, and then you can head to Johnson's spread and break the bad news. We'll try to keep Gordon out of it as long as we can."

Matt nodded and said, "Sounds like a good plan. But be careful. Whoever is responsible for this may be in town keeping an eye out for discovery of the body and what happens after. I don't think I'd say anything to the deputy until you're out of town and on your way back. Do you think you can get him out of town without telling him why?"

Clay smiled and said, "I think so. My days on 'the ol' plantation' taught me to be closemouthed and keep an eye on my backside. If anyone is going to take a shot at my butt, I want you to be near enough so you can make certain they don't."

"You have my word on it." Matt laughed. "And if they should get in a lucky shot, I'll drive you around in a surrey until you're able to ride again."

"I'll hold you to it." Clay smiled and turned his mount and headed for town.

Matt watched until he was out of sight and then started surveying the area around Johnson and the pile of brush. All signs had been thoroughly obliterated by brush having been dragged over the ground. He returned to the body and removed more of the branches from around it. He noticed a couple of furrows where Johnson's feet had been before they had turned him over to look at his face. *He must have been shot elsewhere and dragged here,* Matt thought, and he began to move in the direction the furrows indicated.

He came to the narrow trail that led toward town and saw a piece of metal on the other side. He reached down and picked it up. It was a decorative concho like one that might be found on a belt or vest. Although it didn't appear to be weathered, there was no way of telling how long it had been there or whether it was connected to Johnson's death, but Matt had never been much of a believer in coincidence, so he put it in his pocket. He found no other tracks or signs that would indicate anything out of the ordinary. Matt returned to where Johnson's body was, squatted on his heels, fished out the makings, and rolled himself a smoke.

Why was Johnson murdered? Matt began to consider various possibilities. He knew that Culbertson wanted the Johnson ranch, but would he resort to murder and then confront Maria with a phony deed? Maybe he had won big at cards and someone bushwhacked him for the money. Maybe Johnson had an enemy that simply seized an opportunity when it arose. Matt realized that such speculation was futile. He was a newcomer and simply didn't have the necessary knowledge to come up with any answers at this time. Matt also knew that it was going to take him a little longer to reach the ranch he had recently purchased on a whim, sight unseen. He had been treated with kindness by this dead man's daughter, and Matt knew that he was going to stay around until the mystery of Johnson's death was unraveled.

He was on his second smoke, trying to figure out how best to break the news to Maria, when he heard horses coming along the trail. He stood up as Clay and another rider pulled off the trail and dismounted.

"Earl Burns," Clay said, "meet Matthew Stoker. He was with me when we found the body."

Matt shook hands with the young man. Not as tall as Matt, Burns was well built with light brown hair and blue eyes, and, though young, his face was weathered from the sun. Matt guessed that the deputy did not spend his time lolling around the sheriff's office or the Lucky Lady Saloon.

"Pleased to meet you, Deputy."

"I been hearin' 'bout you," Burns said. "None of it good."

"I can imagine. After all, I was in town long enough to give Aphrodite here a blow and some oats in the livery stable, have some coffee and pie at the café, and have a beer at the Lucky Lady. You would have really gotten an earful if I had taken the time to go to the general store for supplies. Lucky for you, I decided that Twin Forks had had enough excitement for one day."

Clay laughed and Burns smiled, nodded, and moved past Matt to look at the body.

"Damn! It's old man Johnson, all right. This is going to tear Maria apart. She's going to hate me when I tell her. Looks like he was shot in the back. How am I ever going to be able to tell her that her father was shot in the back?" Earl turned to both of them. "You guys better get the body into town and tell the sheriff what you know. I don't know how, but I'm going to have to go out to the ranch and tell Maria that her father's dead."

"Hold on a minute, Deputy," Matt said. "As you've already indicated, I'm not very high in Sheriff Gordon's opinion. What do you think he's going to do when he sees a body brought in by Clay and me? How likely is he to believe anything I say, with Clay being the only other witness? I'm not crazy about your town in the first place, and I certainly have no desire to be buried there."

Matt then proceeded to tell the deputy about his arrival at the ranch, his return when he saw Culbertson and his men riding in, the deed that Culbertson had, Maria's revelation that the deed was worthless, and Matt's subsequent departure for town in an attempt to find Maria's father. When he had finished, Matt paused for a minute to let it all sink in, and then he said, "I think that you and Clay should take Mr. Johnson's body into town. I'll go to the ranch and break the news to Miss Johnson. In the morning you can bring her father out, along with a preacher if you have one, and we'll bury him wherever Miss Johnson wants. While you're in town, keep your eyes open. Whoever's responsible for Johnson's murder is probably waiting around for the body to be discovered. Pay attention to anyone quick to point blame at the notorious gunfighter who had been in town earlier. More often than not, the person who's quickest to accuse someone else has something to hide."

Clay said, "What Matt says makes sense, Earl. It seems to me that the fake deed and where it came from are more likely to lead us to Mr. Johnson's killer. I'm not saying Mr. Culbertson is involved, but I figure that maybe someone who wants to curry his favor is."

"I don't like Maria being out there alone. I don't know that I trust this fellow here to be alone with her," Burns said.

"I understand your concern, Deputy," Matt said, "and I admire you for it, but if my thoughts about Miss Johnson weren't honorable, I would have already had the opportunity to take advantage of the situation. Besides, I left a friend of mine with her when I came to town, and I can assure you that she would never allow anyone, even me, to do harm to the young woman."

Then Matt smiled and added, "I'll inform Miss Johnson of your concern, Deputy."

"I don't like it, but I'll go along with it," Earl said. "But I wish I could be there for her when she hears of her father's death."

"I'll tell her how much you wanted to be with her and how much you care about her," Matt said.

With that, he turned and mounted the Appaloosa. "I'll see you tomorrow. It's probably best that no one knows where I am for the time being."

Clay and Earl watched him ride off. Then they set about building a travois to transport the body into town.

Chapter Seven

As Clay and the deputy were riding back to town, Earl asked, "Is that guy Stoker as bad as they say?"

Clay shook his head. "I don't think so. He stood up to Culbertson out at the Johnson spread, and then he came into town looking for Maria's daddy. He didn't kill Billy Bronson after Billy tried to draw on him. He waited by Johnson's body when he knew I was coming back with a deputy. I think he's good at what he does, but I don't think he takes particular pleasure in it. No, I don't think he's bad. I think he's a good man saddled with a terrible talent."

"Well, I know Sheriff Gordon sure doesn't like him. He told me if I so much as see him spit in public, I should put him behind bars."

"I notice he told you to do it rather than him." Clay laughed. "I guess he figured it would be better if you got gunned down trying to take Matt in rather than himself."

Earl said, "I wouldn't go that far, Clay."

"Well, all I know, Earl, is Gordon had the opportunity to try to arrest him in the Lucky Lady and passed on it.

And to tell you the truth, I don't think Matt would've put up a fight. I think he would've gone along quietly."

"You're probably right, Clay," Earl said, "but I still don't like the fact that he's out there with Maria when she's all alone."

"You know what, Earl?" Clay asked. "I think you're jealous."

Earl muttered, "Am not."

Clay chuckled. It was too dark to see, but he knew that the young deputy was blushing.

They rode the rest of the way into town in silence. Their entrance evoked interest from those who saw them ride in, and by the time they got to the sheriff's office, quite a crowd was gathering. Earl dismounted and went inside. He came out a few seconds later, followed by the sheriff. Gordon moved to the body, looked it over, and nodded.

"That's Johnson, all right," he said. "Where's that gun-fighter? This looks like his work."

"I don't think so, Sheriff," Earl said. "He could have left before Clay and me got there. Besides, the body looked like it had been there a while, and someone had gone to a lot of trouble to brush away all signs."

"That's just the sort of thing that clever bastard would have done to throw us off the track," Gordon said.

"Yeah," said the deputy, "but Clay here was with him when they found the body, and he said the signs had been brushed away when they got there."

The sheriff glowered at his deputy. "I wouldn't put much stock in the word of a no-good, shiftless no-account. Now, you get the body down to Fred Drummond's and have him put together a coffin for Johnson. Where's the gun-fighter now?"

"Last I saw him was where we found Johnson's body," Earl said. He picked up the reins of his horse and started down the street on foot. Clay followed along. Neither man spoke. When they got to Drummond's barbershop, Fred was standing out front.

"Hey, Fred," Earl said.

"Looks like you need some of my carpentry work, Earl," Fred said. "Who is it?"

"Henry Johnson. Got himself bushwhacked," Earl replied.

"Hell, that's a shame. I liked Henry. Both him and his daughter seemed like good folks. Well, give me about an hour, and I'll have him packaged up for you," Fred said. "Who did it? That gunfighter I heard was in town?"

"We don't know who done it, but the sheriff seems certain that it was him."

After carrying Johnson's body into the back room, Earl and Clay headed over to the livery stable, unhooked the travois, and groomed and fed their horses. Then Earl led Clay around to the back door of the Lucky Lady, where he got the bartender to bring them a couple of beers. They sat at the foot of the stairs that led up to the second floor and sipped their brews in silence. Finally, Earl broke the silence.

"I don't understand why Sheriff Gordon wouldn't at least listen to what you had to say, Clay."

"You know the sheriff sees me as less than a varmint, Earl," Clay said. "Besides, he wants Matt to be the one that did it. Makes his life a whole lot easier. There have been no other strangers in town other than members of families heading west and staying down by the river, so if Matt didn't do it, that means it was someone local or one of those homesteaders. And if that's the case, Gordon doesn't really want to know who it was because if it was one of the homesteaders, they've probably already moved on out of the county, and if it was someone local, it more 'an likely would lead to Culbertson's doorstep."

"Yeah, and it's certain that the sheriff don't want to upset that man," Earl said. "I've seen him go a great distance out of his way to avoid ruffling Culbertson's feathers. But I just wouldn't feel right if an innocent man was to be blamed for Johnson's death, and I don't believe Stoker did it."

"I don't either," Clay said. "But I wouldn't worry too much about it. I believe Mr. Stoker can probably hold his own against the sheriff or Mr. Culbertson."

They finished off their beers, and Earl took the mugs back to the bar. In an effort to avoid answering questions from curious townspeople, they crossed the street and walked down to the sheriff's office the back way and entered the alley alongside the jail. As they neared the front of the building, they heard the voice of Curly Williams, Culbertson's foreman, through the open window.

"Look, this is the chance we've been waiting for. We can scatter the stock, tear down some fences, even burn down the barn. It'll be easy to scare Johnson's daughter off the place. Hell, by the time we're through, she'll sell out to Culbertson at any price."

"All right. Go ahead," Sheriff Gordon said. "But I didn't hear any of this. You understand? No one can know I was aware of anything that's going on. After all, I'm the law in this county."

Everyone in the room laughed.

Clay grabbed Earl's arm and dragged him back down the alley. "I'm going to head out to the Johnsons' and let Matt know what they're planning. I don't know why the sheriff is going along with what they're getting ready to do, but it's pretty clear he isn't about to do anything to prevent it," he said quietly.

"Well, I'm certainly not going to be a party to what we just heard," Earl replied. "I'm going with you. Maybe the sheriff is going to stand by and let things happen, but I'm not. Maria could get hurt. We'll get a packhorse from the stable and take Mr. Johnson with us."

"But you're a deputy sheriff," Clay said.

"That's right. And I'm going to do my part to see that the law is upheld. Even if it costs me my job."

Chapter Eight

Maria was sitting at the piano, playing. She finished, spun around on the stool, and said, "What did you think, Drella?"

The dog lay on the floor with her head on her paws, her ears back along her head, and her eyes mournfully on Maria.

"Everyone's a critic. Well, if you don't like Mozart, maybe you'll like this." Maria turned back to the piano and banged out a boisterous version of "Turkey in the Straw."

Drella got up, wagging her tail, and moved over next to Maria. "Oh-ho, so that's the kind of girl you are. I envy you. Sometimes, I wish I could run away and become a dance hall queen." Maria laughed. "But then I think, who would want to buy me a drink? You, on the other hand, could probably get anything you wanted."

Maria got down on her knees beside the dog, put her arms around Drella's neck, and gave her a big hug. "You're such a sweet thing and so much fun to have around. I

haven't played this piano in months. My mother taught me, you know. When we started out from Ohio, I remember my mother saying to my father that he had to find room in the wagon for her piano or she wouldn't go. She said that with the piano, wherever we went we would always be able to stay in touch with civilization and culture."

Maria sat down on the floor beside the dog, and Drella put her head in Maria's lap. "You would've liked my mother, and she would've loved you. She was so beautiful. She was a schoolteacher. She loved music and literature and philosophy, and she taught me to love them too. I miss her, Drella. She came down with fever when we were miles from anywhere. It took her seven days to die, and in all that time we couldn't find any place or anyone to help. After she died, my father wrapped her in a tarpaulin and we traveled day and night until he found this place. When he saw the big oak tree halfway up the small knoll out back, he announced that this was the place for her to rest. He buried her at the foot of that tree and told me that this was going to be our new home. The next day, we rode over the hill and saw the town of Twin Forks. Father found a land office and discovered that the land where we had buried mother was open range. He paid the filing fee for two sections and had me sign as the owner. He told me that that way I wouldn't have to go through the courts when he passed on. It was early spring, and there was still snow on the ground, although much of it had melted. By the end of July, he had built this house, and by the end of September, he had started a small herd of fifteen mavericks and wild strays. The day he finished the house, he gave me a pouch of seeds and told me that my mother had wanted flowers around the house and had brought the seeds from Ohio. That's why there are so many displays here in the house. It was almost as if the seeds were meant for this soil. Oh, Drella, I don't know why I'm telling you all of this. I guess your gentle and loving nature reminds me of her."

Suddenly Drella's ears went up, as did the hairs on the back of her neck, and a growl rumbled quietly in her throat. The dog got up and turned toward the door.

Maria rose and went to the window. Through the dusk she could make out a rider dismounting in the yard and heading for the house. She picked up the Winchester and opened the door. The man had just made it to the top of the steps leading to the porch. He saw the rifle and stopped. Maria recognized him as one of Culbertson's hands. He wasn't a big man, but he had a rugged look about him. His nose looked as if it had been broken, and there was a scar on the side of his face. He took off his hat and said, "Evenin', ma'am. My name is Ed Rivers. As you've probably guessed, I was told to keep an eye on your place by Mr. Culbertson. I've been settin' in that grove of trees up yonder for most of the afternoon and evening. I heard ya playin' the pianee and thought I would come down and see if I could scrounge a cup of coffee and listen to ya play awhile."

"I won't deny a man a cup of coffee," Maria said. "You wait right there and I'll bring you a cup." Maria backed away and started to close the door. In a flash, the man shoved the door open with his shoulder, grabbed the rifle, pushed Maria back into the house, and kicked the door closed. He caught hold of her blouse and started to rip it off, but just then he was hit by a snarling and snapping eighty pounds. Drella knocked him to the floor. The man yelled in surprise and struggled against the dog's ferocious attack. Finally, he grabbed her by the scruff of the neck and hurled her across the room. He pulled his Colt and took aim at the dog.

"No!" Maria screamed.

The man glanced in her direction and then turned his attention back to the dog, who was getting ready to spring at him again.

"Pull the trigger and you're a dead man," a voice behind him said softly but firmly, and then, "Drella, sit. Stay."

The man looked over his shoulder and saw Matt standing in the doorway, his Colt still in his holster. He started to turn, but the voice caused him to pause.

"You'll never make it, but if you feel the need to try, go ahead," Matt said.

The man hesitated a moment and then whirled and fired, but he was a split second too late. Matt's shot hit him in the head, causing him to fall backward and causing the bullet from his pistol to go into the ceiling. Maria screamed and covered her face at the sight of blood and gray matter splattered on the wall. Matt moved to the body and kicked the Colt out of reach, just out of habit. Then, he turned to Maria.

"Are you all right?" he asked.

She was pale and trembling, but she nodded her head. "Everything happened so fast. I should have known better, but he took me by surprise, and then when Drella jumped in to protect me and he drew his gun and was going to shoot her—I screamed." She paused and took in everything around her. Maria shuddered and started sobbing. "I've seen death before, but nothing like this. I know you didn't have a choice, but it's so horrible," she said to Matt.

"Okay, Drella," Matt said. The dog, who had been sitting since Matt had told her to, went over to Maria and nuzzled her hand.

Maria dropped to her knees and put her arms around the dog. "Oh, Drella, I don't know what would have happened to me if you hadn't been here. I'm sure you saved my life." Then she looked at Matt. "Both of you."

"I don't know," Matt said. "I have a feeling that the two of you young ladies would have done okay for yourselves."

"He was going to shoot Drella," Maria said.

"Drella's been shot at before. I don't think he would have hit her. But I admit I'm just as glad he didn't get the chance. We've been best friends far too long for me to get along without her. She has saved my bacon more than once. Isn't that right, big girl?" Matt reached down and scratched Drella behind the ear. The dog wagged her tail and licked Matt's hand.

"Well, I think I'd better get our friend here out of the house and then try to clean this place up a bit," Matt said and moved over to the body. He looked at the dead man. "Wasn't he one of the riders with Culbertson?"

"Yes, I think he was," Maria replied. "When he came to the door, he told me that Mr. Culbertson had told him to keep track of what was going on here."

"Well, I'll wrap him up and put him and his horse in the barn. Then tomorrow I'll return him to Culbertson."

Matt picked up the dead man and put him over his shoulder. He also reached down and picked up the man's hat and Colt and then went out the door. The dog started to follow, but Matt raised a hand, signaling her to stay.

"Good girl," Matt said and then, wanting to get Maria's mind off of what had just happened, asked, "Got any coffee?"

Maria turned to the stove and put the pot on. She also put on some water to heat and got some rags that she kept for cleaning. "When I'm through cleaning up the mess here," she said to Drella, "I will probably collapse, so don't you worry if you see me fall to the floor."

Drella cocked her head to the side and looked at Maria as if she understood every word. That look put a smile on Maria's face just for a moment. Then she grimaced and turned to the task at hand.

In the barn, Matt found a tarpaulin and wrapped it around the body. He put Aphrodite and the other horse in stalls, stripped the gear from them, and put a halter on the dead man's horse and secured it to the stall. He gave both animals a helping of hay and oats. He got the brush and curry comb from his saddlebags and began to work on the Appaloosa.

"We've had a hell of a day, Aphro, haven't we? I am truly tired of it all. When we get to our ranch, I'm going to make it a place where we can settle down. Maybe there, we can put it all behind us."

The horse stopped her eating, turned her head, and looked at him. "I know, I know. Stop talking and keep brushing. There's no question that you are a beautiful girl, but you are somewhat weak in the compassion department."

Matt finished with Aphrodite and went back to the house. He noticed that the floor and wall had already been cleaned. Maria told him to sit at the table. "I'm certain you won't mind a little stew and biscuits with your coffee," she said as she put a plate down in front of him, along with a cup of hot coffee.

"How could you know that I haven't eaten anything but a slice of apple pie since the last meal you fixed for me? Aren't you going to join me?"

"Drella and I had our supper earlier," Maria said. "Besides, after tonight, I don't think I will ever eat again. It was just so awful."

"You should have left the cleaning up for me. What with the war and everything, I've been exposed to such things before," Matt said. "However, I think you better sit down anyway. I need to talk to you."

The tone of his voice made Maria shiver, and she sat down at the table and placed her hands in her lap so that he wouldn't see that they were trembling. "It's about Daddy, isn't it?"

"I'm afraid so. There is no easy way to say it, Maria. Your father is dead."

Maria let out a shriek and brought her hands to her face. Then she started to cry. At the sound of Maria's crying,

Drella got up. She went to Maria and nuzzled her arm. Maria dropped one hand and absently stroked the dog's head. "What happened? How did it happen? When?"

"I have no answers for you. Clay Harper said your father came to the stable late last night, got his horse, and said he was going to head down to the creek to get some sleep before he headed home. Clay and I rode out to see if he was still around. We had about given up when we found him. He had been shot in the back and covered over with brush. Clay went to town and got the deputy sheriff, Earl Burns. He's going to bring your father out in the morning. We'll bury him wherever you say. As to who did it, there's no evidence, but given the phony deed, I can think of a good candidate."

"Murdered? Oh, my god. But Mr. Culbertson wouldn't do that. He wants our land, sure, but I can't believe he would resort to murder," Maria said. "He has always been courteous and, in some ways, kind to us."

"Maybe so. But he seems to be a hard man. He was willing to let one of his hands go up against me in town. He was just a boy, and I'm fairly sure that Culbertson knew the kid wouldn't have had a chance against me, but he didn't do anything to try to stop it," Matt said, and he told her what had occurred.

Maria just sat there, considering everything she had heard. Suddenly, tears welled up in her eyes, and she rushed from the table into her bedroom. Matt slowly finished the supper that had been put before him. He went out on the porch, rolled a smoke, and listened to the gentle sounds of the evening. He crushed out the embers and went back inside. Drella was curled in a corner, but her eyes were open. When Matt came in, she yawned and closed her eyes. Matt smiled. He knew that the dog had been keeping watch over the young woman of the house. He walked over to the piano and sat. His hands found the keyboard, and he began to play. After a few moments, Maria came to the doorway of her room and listened until he finished the piece.

"That was beautiful," she said, still dabbing at her eyes. "Debussy, wasn't it?"

Matt nodded. "It's been a while. I learned to play from my grandmother back in Virginia. She was a remarkable woman. She taught me to appreciate the arts. She also taught me to read Greek and Latin. I loved the plays of Sophocles and the epic poems of Homer and Virgil. I've read the plays and poetry of Shakespeare, the poetry of Pope and Wordsworth, and I particularly enjoy many of our own writers, like Cooper, Hawthorne, Irving, and Poe. My grandmother would always tell me that to really learn about the world and the people in it, I should read the works of the best writers of any age. Then came the war, and after the war came the man sitting at your piano. I don't think my grandmother would be very pleased with what I've become or how I've invested her educational efforts."

"I think she would be very proud," Maria said. "She would know that it's not what a man does, but what a man is. And I know that, like my father, her grandson is a very good man, indeed."

"I'm not so sure, but thank you for saying so."

A low rumble came from Drella. "Good girl. I hear them," Matt said, and he got up and went to the window.

"It's Clay and Deputy Burns. I think they have your father with them."

Maria rushed to the window, and then she looked down at her blouse that was torn at the shoulder. She ran into her bedroom, and when she returned she was wearing a different blouse. Matt smiled.

"Earl Burns is a nice-looking young man."

Maria blushed a bit. "I simply didn't want anyone to get the wrong idea."

As they stepped out on the porch, Matt asked if she was all right, and Maria nodded that she was. The riders pulled up in the front yard.

"I thought you were going to wait until morning," Matt said as the two men swung down from their saddles.

"Something came up, and we figured we better get out here as soon as possible," Clay said.

"Earl, why don't you go on inside and have some coffee. Clay and I will look to the stock."

"If that's my father," Maria said, nodding toward the coffin on the back of the packhorse, "I would appreciate it if you would take him into his bedroom. It doesn't seem fitting to leave him in the barn overnight."

Earl and Clay carried Henry Johnson into the house and did as Maria asked. They returned to the porch. Clay took off his hat and said, "I'm terribly sorry, Miss Johnson."

"Thank you, Clay," she said. "I appreciate everything you and Earl have done. You both must be starved. Come inside. There's coffee and stew."

"I'll be there in a few minutes, ma'am," Clay said.

Maria led Earl into the house, while Matt and Clay took

the horses into the barn. Clay looked at the tarp that had been wrapped around the Culbertson hand.

"You been busy. Anyone I know?"

"Probably. He rides for the Circle C," Matt said, and told Clay what had happened. They stripped the gear from the horses and supplied them with a helping of grain and alfalfa. Then Matt led the way back to the house.

When they walked through the door, Clay jumped to one side. "Lord almighty! What's that?" he asked, pointing at Drella.

Matt laughed. "That's my friend, Cinderella. Drella for short. Her job is to see that these young people don't start fooling around. Drella, come on over and say hello."

While Maria blushed and Earl looked down and drew a circle on the floor with the toe of his boot, Drella got up, wagging her tail, went over to Clay, and nudged his hand.

"I know what you want," Clay said, and he reached down and scratched her on the rump. Drella took the treatment with dignity and exhibited no desire to move away.

"She'll stay there all day as long as you keep scratching," Matt said. "Come on over and have a seat and some coffee, and you can tell us why you felt the need to come out this evening."

Everyone moved to the table, and Maria set cups and the coffeepot in the center. She also supplied plates of stew for the new arrivals. When they were seated, and after much of the stew had disappeared, Clay told them about what had happened in town. When he finished, everyone just sat there for a moment, digesting what had been said. Finally, Maria spoke up.

"Nobody is going to run me off this place, no matter what they do. My mother is buried here and now my father will be too. I'm staying even if it means that I'll be laid alongside them."

"I don't think that's going to happen," Matt said. "It sounds to me like they simply want to run you off. Still, as things escalate, anything can happen. Somehow we have to bring this to a halt before matters get out of hand." Then he looked at Earl. "What about you? You're the law. What kind of hand are you going to play?"

"I'm siding with Maria," he said. "When Gordon finds out, I doubt I'll be a deputy anymore, but what he's doing is wrong, and I don't want any part of it."

Matt looked at Clay.

"Hey, I'm here, ain't I? I am not overly fond of Twin Forks, and I'm fairly certain that I can get a job mucking out stables and swamping saloons almost anywhere. Hell, after what I heard, I packed my saddlebags and tied up all my other gear in my blanket," Clay said, "and I can't say that I'd be sorry to leave this part of the country."

"All right, we need a plan. Between the four of us, we have to stay aware of what's happening and try to prevent any further harm coming this way. Maria, where's your stock located?" Matt asked.

"They were moved to the high pasture just last week. Daddy hired some extra help, and we did the branding and drove them up to the meadow. It's about a mile west of here," she answered.

"All right," Matt said. "First thing in the morning, we will see that Maria's father is given a proper burial and . . ."

Suddenly, Maria broke into tears and bolted from the room. Earl leaped up and started after her, but Matt held up his hand and stopped him. They could hear deep, heart-wrenching sobs coming from the bedroom. Earl returned to his chair, and the three of them sat there in silence. Finally, the crying stopped, and a few minutes later Maria came back to the table and sat down. Her eyes were red and puffy, but she appeared to have her emotions under control.

"With all that's happened today, I guess that it never really hit me until just now that Daddy is dead," she explained. "You were saying that we'll bury him in the morning. Then what?"

Matt said gently, "I think we should leave the rest until morning. We're all a little tired, and our thinking will be clearer after we get some rest. The three of us will sleep in the barn. I'll leave Drella here with you."

He got up, and the others followed suit, muttering their good nights. At the door, Matt turned to Maria.

"I'm sorry. You've been given more in a single day than any one person should have to put up with in a lifetime. And I'd hate to see anything added to it, so given what Clay and Earl overheard, if anything happens tonight, I want you to stay inside and do nothing. Don't go reaching for your Winchester figuring to help. We'll take care of it. From what they said, they're only going to try to scare you. I don't want any more killing around here, and if killing becomes necessary, I don't want you doing it. Do you understand?"

Maria nodded her head.

"Promise you'll stay inside and keep out of it?"

"I promise."

"Good. Try to get some sleep. Drella, stay. Guard."

Matt went into the barn where Clay and Earl were busy spreading their blankets.

"That is one remarkably strong woman," Clay said.

Matt nodded in agreement.

"I've known that for a long time," Earl said. Then, indicating the tarpaulin, he asked, "What's that all about?"

Matt told him about the situation he'd walked into when he returned to the ranch. When he finished, he could see that Earl was very agitated.

"It's okay, son," Matt said. "She wasn't hurt. And I'm here to tell you that that is one strong woman. She's been through all sorts of hell today, and she still found time to feed us. She has shown more courage and heart than I could have under similar circumstances."

"It just riles me," Earl said. "If something had happened, the damned sheriff wouldn't have done a thing. Hell, he probably would've tried to blame that on you too."

"Well, it's over now," Clay said, "and we've got more pressing problems." He turned to Matt. "How do you want to handle it? Take turns keeping watch?"

"Yes, we'll each take two-hour shifts," Matt said. "If something or someone comes up, whoever's on watch will wake the others. I'll take the first shift. I want you both to realize one thing. Whatever may or may not happen, the problems Maria is facing are not going to be resolved by our actions tonight. If they come, let's be very careful in what we do. If what you told us is true, they don't plan to do any real harm at first. They just want to try to scare

Maria into selling out and leaving. Our best course of action may be to lay low and do nothing. If they don't know that we're here or how many of us there are, it could work in our favor later on."

Matt went to the window in the tack room and opened it. "There's a good view of the front yard from here." He walked back to his gear and slipped his carbine out of the scabbard. Then he picked up an empty crate, carried it over to the window, and sat.

"I know with everything that's happened," Matt said, "it'll be hard to get any sleep, but we have to try."

"You're right. It will be hard," Clay said. "Hopefully nothing at all will happen. Lord knows we all could use the rest." He turned out the lantern, and the two men crawled into their blankets.

Matt rolled himself a smoke, turned away from the window, and lit it. He wasn't worried about anyone smelling the smoke. He figured if they came tonight, they would come in hard and loud. More than likely, they would have been drinking earlier. Men like this always tended to find their courage in John Barleycorn. They wouldn't expect anyone to be watching for them. Matt was convinced that the greatest danger would come from an accident, a stray shot hitting someone or sparking a fire. If he could keep those who were behind this from knowing how many were helping Maria Johnson, Matt was certain that the element of surprise would prove to be of great benefit later. If they came tonight, the best thing that could happen would be for Clay, Earl, and him not to have to reveal their presence.

Matt rolled another smoke and let his mind drift back over the last few days. In heading for his new ranch, he had tried to stay off the main routes in an attempt to avoid any confrontations. Now, here he was in the middle of he knew not what. *Just for a drink of well water for the animals and myself,* he thought. Well, now it was much more, and what troubled him was that he really didn't know the players or whether or not the deck was stacked.

Matt started listing in his mind the questions to which he had no answers. Was Culbertson really the villain in this little play? Maria didn't seem to think so. Was the sheriff really crooked or simply a man looking after his own best interests? Who had murdered Henry Johnson and why? Were the hands of the Circle C acting on their own because they thought that was what Culbertson would want, or were they under orders—and if so, whose? Matt knew he needed to get some answers if he had any hope of avoiding wholesale bloodshed.

He was about to build yet another smoke when he heard horses approaching. He quickly rousted the others and moved back to the window. They saw a group of riders down by the end of the corral. Suddenly, they charged in, yelling and firing into the air. Earl drew his Colt and started to aim through the window. Matt reached out and pushed his hand down before he could get a shot off.

"They're just making noise," Matt whispered. "Let's not let them know we're here unless we have to."

The riders milled around in front of the house yelling and shooting and then turned and rode off. One of them turned back and shouted, "If you know what's good for you, you'll pack up and get out before you get hurt!" Then he too turned and rode off.

Matt, Clay, and Earl came out of the barn, and Earl ran to the front door. "Maria, are you all right?" he called.

Matt quickly looked in the direction of the riders, but they were too far off to hear the deputy.

"Earl Burns, quit raising a ruckus. I'm fine," Maria said as she opened the door. "Drella woke me before they even started. She and I just lay on the floor and listened till their hell-raising was over."

Clay turned to Matt, smiled, and said, "Ain't love grand?"

Matt laughed and shook his head. "I do believe our Leander has found his Hero, and he didn't even have to swim the Hellespont."

The four of them stood in the yard, looking in the direction that the riders had taken. Finally, Matt suggested that they all try to get some sleep. "I don't figure there'll be any more excitement tonight."

Chapter Nine

The first streaks of light were spreading across the eastern sky when Matt came out of the barn. He walked down to the stream that ran by the north side of the house and went along it until he found a small pool. He stripped down and bathed himself in the icy water. Refreshed, he dressed and wandered around back and up a small hill. He had noticed the grave yesterday when he had returned because of Culbertson's arrival. There was a nice view of the valley, and he figured this would be where Maria would want her father buried. He turned at the sound of footsteps and saw Maria approaching with a small bouquet of flowers. She moved past him and knelt and placed them at the head of the grave. She bowed her head for a few moments, and then rose and turned to Matt.

"My mother," she said. "Now she and Daddy can be together again. I think he has wanted that for a long time."

Matt nodded and said nothing.

"Well, aren't you an early bird," Maria observed. "Come on down to the house. The coffee should be ready."

They walked back to the house together, and Maria indicated the table, where Matt took a seat. She poured two cups of coffee, and, giving him one, she sat down.

"Are you all right?" Matt asked.

Maria shook her head. "No, but there's not a damned thing I can do about it, is there? But I'll tell you one thing, Matthew Stoker. I'm not leaving. My mother is buried up on that knoll, and soon my father will be, and when I die, I will be too."

Her eyes glistened with the suggestion of tears, but Matt also saw determination and commitment in them.

"I will do everything in my power to see that you have a long life of many happy years before taking your place beside them," he said.

She smiled at him. "Whatever did I do to be worthy of having a knight in shining armor looking after me?"

Matt almost choked on his coffee. "I'm no knight, believe me. I'm just a man passing through. I'm good with a gun and good at what I do. I have a set of values morally and, I believe, a good sense of right and wrong ethically. I've never gone against either, but I assure you I am no knight. Now, Earl Burns, there's a champion. If anyone is cut out to be worthy of bearing lance and shield, he's the one."

Maria blushed, and asked, "How does a man get started in your line of work? It doesn't seem to fit with the type of person I see sitting at my table."

"Oh, I don't know. You can't say you really know the man sitting at your table."

"Maybe not, but I do know he didn't start out as a hired gun."

Matt smiled. "That's true enough. But my father taught me how to use one when I was very young, and when I was older the war taught me how to use one to kill people, and I became very good at it. The war also took away everything I valued in life, so I turned to what I could do well and found that I could make a pretty good living at it. Not a lot of friends, but the best hotels and good food. Funny, though, I recently purchased a small spread. That's where I was headed when I rode in here. I was hoping that I could put my gun away and settle down, but maybe that's just a dream. Maybe a leopard can't change his spots."

"I think you're a man who can do whatever he wants," Maria said. "I believe that you will put your gun down and make a new life. I'm just sorry that my problems got in your way." Matt started to speak, but she put up her hand to stop him. "I better get started on breakfast," she said, getting up from the table and moving to the stove.

Matt got up. "I'll go stir the others out of their blankets." He poured some more coffee in his cup. "If the smell of your coffee doesn't rouse them, nothing will."

He started for the door, but Maria stopped him as he opened it. "Matthew, thank you. You've done so much. I truly appreciate it."

"No thanks are necessary, Maria. I'm just doing what I have to do. It's my nature. If you want to thank me, give me a flower to remember you by when I leave." He smiled and closed the door.

They were all sitting around the table finishing up with breakfast. Clay pushed his chair back a little, placed his hands on his stomach, and said, "That's the best breakfast I've had since the last time my mother cooked one for me. Thank you, Miss Johnson."

"You're quite welcome, Clay, and it's Maria," she said. "I'm very flattered to have my cooking compared to your mother's. While my mother taught me to cook, I know that I'm nowhere near as good a cook as she was. I think it's a rule. All mothers cook better than their offspring."

Everyone chuckled, and Matt poured himself more coffee. "Okay then, let's get down to business. We need to find out what's going on. Who the good guys are and who the bad. After we place Maria's father next to her mother, I want you, Clay, to head to the upper pasture and look to the beef. I'm going to take the package in the barn back to the Circle C, and Earl, I want you to stay and keep an eye on things here. Any questions?"

"Yeah," Clay said. "What do you want me to do if I see someone messin' with the cattle?"

"Just fire a shot in the air," Matt said. "I don't think any of these guys are seriously into being rustlers. I think they're merely trying to harass. If they should come at you, don't try to stay and fight. Head on back here. Two guns are better than one."

"Three," Maria said.

Matt looked at her quizzically.

"Three guns," she said. "And don't give me any arguments."

"No, ma'am," Matt said. "Wouldn't think of it. How about you, Earl? Any questions?"

Earl shook his head. "No, I think it's the best we can

do with our current numbers. Still, I don't think it's a good idea to go to Culbertson's alone."

"I won't be alone," Matt replied. "Drella will come along with me. The two of us have handled more difficult situations. Haven't we, girl? Besides, if they want to take me out, another gun or two won't make any difference. By coming in alone, I don't think anyone will start anything without Culbertson's say-so."

None of them liked it, but they nodded in agreement.

"Right, then. Let's get started," Matt said. "Maria, you wait here until we get everything ready."

"All right," she said, "but I would like to see my father one last time."

Matt nodded and followed the others out.

The three men dug the grave and carried the coffin up the hill. Drella lay under the tree with her head on her paws. Clay loosened the top and slid it down just far enough so that Maria could see her father but not his wound. Matt nodded to Earl, who went down to get Maria.

"This is never an easy time, is it?" Clay said.

"Death is never easy," said Matt, "particularly when it's a close family member. But this one is harder still because it was so cowardly and senseless."

"Are your parents still alive?" Clay asked.

"My mother is. She and my sister are living in New York. My father died during the war trying to defend our home. It's funny. War always seems to be harder on those who stay behind. I guess from your point of view the war was a necessity, and if I were a slave, I would feel the same.

But I've thought about it a good deal, and I'll be damned if I can see that many problems were solved by the conflict between the North and the South. The colored folk don't seem to be a whole lot better off than they were before."

"Maybe not," Clay replied, "but at least we're free."

"There's that," Matt said. "What about your folks, Clay? Are they still living?"

"My mother died during the war. A confederate soldier shot her because she wouldn't stop tending to a wounded Northern boy. I killed him with my bare hands and then ran off. I guess I've been running ever since."

"And your father?"

"I never really knew him. He was sold to another plantation owner when we were first brought here. I wanted to look for him but had no idea where to start."

Maria and Earl came around the corner of the house and walked up toward them. Maria carried a bouquet of flowers selected from the flower beds around the house. When they got to the little cemetery, Earl stopped and Maria continued on to the coffin. She removed a single rose from the bouquet and placed it on her father's chest. She also placed a pipe and tobacco pouch in with her father. She knelt there for several minutes. Then she stood, looked at the three men, and nodded. Clay nailed the lid back in place, and they lowered Mr. Henry Johnson into his final resting place. Matt reached for a shovel, but paused when he saw Clay step forward to the edge of the grave.

"Thank you, Mr. Johnson," Clay said. "Every time you came into town you took time to speak to me and ask how I was doing. Of all the people in that town, you insisted on treating me like a man, like a human being. I can't tell you how much that meant to me." Then Clay looked up and said, "Lord, You're getting a very good man. I only hope that when my time comes, I am as worthy as Henry Johnson to enter Your kingdom."

Clay stepped back, and Maria came up beside him and kissed him on the cheek. Matt and Earl began to shovel dirt while Clay escorted Maria back to the house. When they had finished, Matt and Earl also returned to the house, with Drella following behind. Maria poured them coffee and then went to the sideboard and got a bottle and four glasses of fine crystal. She poured a small portion in each glass and said, "I want to thank you for all you've done, but particularly for being here and helping at this time. This was my daddy's favorite brandy, and the crystal glasses were a wedding present from my grandmother to my mother when she married Daddy. I would like you all to join me in drinking a toast to my father."

They all stood and picked up their glasses. "To Henry Johnson," Maria said. "May God rest his soul." And they all drank. "Thank you, again."

Maria turned and went into her bedroom. Matt, Clay, and Earl sat at the table in silence, sipping their coffee. Finally, Matt said, "Well, we have other things to attend to. Earl, I've been thinking. If anyone does show up here at the ranch, it might be better if you keep your eye on things through the window there. You're the nearest thing we have to the law, and the fewer people who know you're here, the better. Also, it might be a good idea if you use that scattergun there in the corner if things start to get touchy. Scatterguns tend to get a person's attention pretty quickly."

Earl walked over, picked up the shotgun, and broke it open.

"Shells are here in the drawer," Maria said, coming in from the bedroom. She got a box of shells from the drawer and handed them to Earl. He loaded two of them into the gun and then propped it next to the window.

Clay got up and started for the door. "If I'm going to ride to the upper pasture, I better get going." He stopped at the door. "Are you all right, ma'am?"

"I'm fine, Clay, and please, it's Maria."

"Okay, Maria."

"I had better be on my way too," Matt said. "You two be careful. I doubt anything will happen today, but don't take any chances. Come on, Drella."

Matt went to the barn and saddled the Appaloosa. Clay had just finished with his roan. He pulled himself into his saddle, turned to Matt, and said, "You be careful, Matthew. There're some hard cases at the Circle C, and don't forget about Billy. You embarrassed him big time. When a young man like that gets embarrassed, there's no telling what he might do."

"I'll keep my eyes open, and don't forget, Drella gives me eyes in the back of my head. You only taking a rifle? I have an extra Colt in my saddlebags if you want it."

"Thanks anyway," Clay said. "I'm fair to middlin' with

a long gun, but I would probably shoot myself in the foot with a handgun." Clay smiled.

Clay rode out, and Matt got the dead ranch hand's horse and tied the body on it. He rode out of the barn leading the Circle C horse, waved to Maria and Earl, and headed for Culbertson's ranch.

Chapter Ten

Clay was enjoying the ride up through the pines toward the high pasture. *This is being free,* he thought, as he watched a four-point buck bounce away from him into the trees. When the war ended, he'd been told he was free, but that had only meant that he could muck out stables and swamp saloon floors and chop firewood for anyone who would pay him. And the pay was not what it would have been if he had been a white man. When he worked for a farmer or rancher, he was often not allowed to sleep in bunkhouses and was told to take his food outside to eat. When he worked in towns, he frequently had to find a place in the livery stable or some outbuilding to sleep, and he had to go to the back doors of restaurants or saloons for his food. None of that was freedom, at least not the sort of freedom others had. Not the sort of freedom he had dreamed about.

But here he was now, riding out on his own. Doing something for someone else, not because he had been told to, but because he wanted to. He was welcome at the same table as the others. He was given the same responsibilities as the others. He was treated like an equal. Now, that was freedom.

He paused in the midst of a stream to let his roan take a drink. He saw a fish jump downstream and remembered how much he enjoyed fishing. He saw a hawk circling overhead and wondered what the freedom of flight would be like. He urged his horse on at a steady trot, watching the various inhabitants of the area scurry about their daily activities, and made a silent vow to himself that, one way or another, he was not going back to a life of mere survival. No, sir, he was going to remain his own man from this point on.

Clay broke through the trees and came to the crest that overlooked a small valley, lush with green grass. "This must be the place, eh, Partner?" he said to the roan.

He saw the cattle at the far end of the valley. Some were grazing, some lying down. Nothing seemed amiss. Clay dismounted, loosened the girth on Partner, pulled his Winchester from the scabbard, and settled himself with his back against a tree. He rolled himself a smoke and sat there, taking in the beauty of the high pasture. *Lord Almighty, the Johnsons sure got themselves a nice piece of land,* he thought, as he snuffed out his smoke, pulled his hat down over his eyes, and dozed off.

He was awakened by the distant sounds of shouting and gunfire. Two drovers were trying to stampede the cattle in his direction. Clay figured they intended to scatter them throughout the trees. Not much damage but a hell of a lot of work finding them all. Clay rose and tightened the girth on the roan in case he had to move out fast. The cattle were moving but not in any real panic.

"Too well fed and rested," Clay muttered as he levered a cartridge into his rifle. When the herd was closer, Clay fired a couple of rounds into the air. The herd began to veer off and start to circle, while the two surprised hands took off for the tree line. Clay fired a couple more shots for effect and watched as the riders disappeared among the pines.

"I guess they weren't expecting us, Partner. I don't think they'll come back, but we'll hang around for a while just to make certain," Clay said. He sat down and leaned against the tree again and rolled himself another smoke. His mind returned to the graveside conversation of this morning. "Never a day goes by that I don't think of Mama," he said to the roan. "You know, Partner, I was very lucky. Mama not only taught me to read and write, but she borrowed all sorts of books from the master's library. She told me to read and learn. She said that what I encountered in books would help me cope with similar situations in real life, and I tell you true, she knew what she was talking about. Many of the stories and poems that I read for pleasure have helped me through a lot of difficult situations and saved me from a great deal of pain. Some folks may think I'm less than they are, but my reading taught me different. I also learned that it's what's inside a man that counts, not what he looks like on the outside."

Clay snuffed out his smoke and reached for the bridle. "Doesn't look like they're coming back, so we might as well head on back to the ranch where we can be of help if anyone comes around stirring up trouble," he said as he swung up into the saddle and turned toward the Johnson place.

Down below, Matt heard the sound of gunfire in the distance: first what sounded like pistol fire, then two rifle shots, followed shortly by two more. He figured the rifle shots were Clay's, and as there were no further shots, Matt assumed that Clay had everything under control. He noticed that Drella was also looking in the direction from which the shots had come.

"It's okay, girl," Matt said. "I think Clay's all right. You like him, don't you, Drella? Well, I do too."

In fact, Matt had been thinking quite a bit about Clay. Matt couldn't understand why the sheriff wouldn't allow Clay to be served in his saloon or why the townspeople would tolerate a person being treated in such a manner.

"You know, Drella," Matt said. Drella perked up her ears and looked up at him. "Maybe we'll ask Clay to join us. You and I aren't going to be able to handle a ranch all by ourselves. Maybe we can talk Clay into coming in with us as a partner. You'd like that, wouldn't you?"

Matt rode on about a mile farther, where he came to a little knoll. Down below, about a half mile away, he saw the ranch house. Matt pulled up and studied the area. After a few moments he said to both horse and dog, "Well, ladies, if they don't want us to leave, we may be in trouble, because I sure don't see any easy way out that offers any protection. I guess we had better be on our best behavior."

With that, he urged the Appaloosa on, while removing

the hammer guard and making sure that the Colt was loose in the holster. As he rode into the front yard and up toward the house, he noticed ranch hands coming from the barn and the bunkhouse. When he reined up in front of the house, the door opened and Culbertson stepped out, flanked by another hand whom Matt recognized as the young man who had tried to brace him in the Lucky Lady. Matt wasn't certain whether or not he had been one of the riders raising hell last night at the Johnson ranch, but he had dealt with the young man's foolish behavior before. Until he knew better, Matt figured that he had better keep an eye on the young hothead.

Matt touched his hat and said, "Good afternoon, Mr. Culbertson."

"What can I do for you, Mr. . . . ?"

"Stoker, Matthew Stoker. You have a very short memory, Mr. Culbertson."

Matt could see that his words struck Culbertson like a slap across the face, but the rancher held himself in check. "As I said, what can I do for you, Mr. Stoker?"

"Well, sir, inasmuch as this fellow here was riding a Circle C horse, I figured he belonged here, so I brought him over," Matt said, indicating the body.

A wrangler walked over and lifted the tarp. "It's Ed Rivers," he said.

"Who killed him?" Culbertson asked.

"I did."

There was a murmur among the hands, and Drella started to growl.

"That growl you hear from my dog tells me that some

of your men are reaching toward their sidearms. If she barks, it'll mean that one or more have their hands on their pistols, at which time I will kill you, Mr. Culbertson, and maybe the fellow next to you and one or two more. I didn't come here for trouble, Mr. Culbertson. I didn't come here to kill, nor to be killed. I came to bring this man to a place where he could be buried and to have a conversation with you. That's all."

Culbertson raised his hand toward his men, indicating that they should hold off. Then he turned his attention back to Matt and asked, "How did Ed die?"

"He was attacking Miss Johnson in her own house, and she has the scratches and torn clothes to prove it," Matt said. "My dog was there and objected to what Rivers was doing. He pulled his sidearm and aimed it at Drella here. I came in at that moment and told him if he pulled the trigger, it would be the last thing he would ever do. He tried to turn the gun on me and didn't make it. I never enjoy shooting a man, Mr. Culbertson, but where I come from men are not allowed to mistreat women in such a fashion."

"It's not something I condone either, Stoker," Culbertson said.

"Maybe that's so, maybe not. I don't know," Matt said to him. "What I do know is that Mr. Henry Johnson was shot in the back, and you have made no secret about trying to get hold of the Johnson ranch. His daughter was attacked by a man who rides for you. She was also visited by night riders last night, yelling and shooting, trying to scare her off her property. I don't know who they were, but it wouldn't surprise me if they aren't standing here in your yard at this moment. And unless I miss my guess, those two riders just coming in were up at Johnson's high pasture this morning trying to run off the stock. A lot of things are happening, and they all seem to point to the Circle C."

"I'm telling you, I had nothing to do with any of this," Culbertson said, his face turning red.

Matt shook his head. "I'm not saying you did, Mr. Culbertson, but I am saying that I'm not moving on until the harassment of Miss Johnson stops. I'm also saying that those five riders last night could easily have joined Ed here. And those two hands walking over from the corral could be lying up in the high pasture. They aren't because I wanted to talk to you first. Now, I've said my piece, and if anything further happens as regards Miss Johnson, I won't waste my time talking."

"Is that a threat?"

"I don't make threats, Mr. Culbertson. I make promises."

With that, Matt turned Aphrodite and started out of the yard at the same pace he had ridden in. Drella followed at the heels of the horse, pausing every few seconds to look back at the men in the yard. After he had gotten beyond the corrals, Matt said, "Okay, Drella. If they were going to shoot us, I think they'd have done it by now," and the dog trotted up alongside.

Chapter Eleven

John Culbertson watched Matt and the dog as they moved off. "That's a hard man," he said to Billy Bronson, who was standing beside him. "But I also suspect he's a man of some honor and not likely to be lying about those activities he mentioned. Do you know anything about the things he said have been going on, Billy?"

"No, sir, Mr. Culbertson!" Billy said. "After I made such a fool of myself in town, I came back to the ranch. I did wake up when Curly and a group of hands came in last night, and they was laughing and carrying on some. I heard Jake Starkweather ask if they was goin' to have a repeat performance tonight, and Curly said that he didn't see why not. But, honest, Mr. Culbertson, I don't know what they was talkin' about."

Culbertson looked at the young man for a minute, nodded, and smiled. "Okay, Billy. Thanks. Would you find Curly and tell him I'd like to see him?"

Culbertson turned and stepped down from the porch.

He walked over to the two men who had just ridden in and put their horses up in the corral.

"Aren't you boys supposed to be in the south pasture helping with the branding?" he asked.

The taller of the two removed his hat and hung his head. "Yes, sir, we was yesterday, but last night Curly told us to go up to Johnson's high pasture and scatter the herd into the trees. He said it would make the Johnson girl more willing to sell her spread."

"And you two didn't see anything wrong with that?"

"Well, sir," the puncher continued, "Curly's the foreman, and I never worked any ranch where you didn't lose your job if you was to tell the foreman you wasn't going to do what he said."

Culbertson understood what the hand was saying. It wasn't a ranch hand's place to challenge the head hand of the outfit. For all these two knew, the orders had come from Culbertson himself. "All right," he said to the two of them. "You get out to the branding and lend a hand." The two men turned to go, but after a few steps, Culbertson stopped them. "If you get an order from anyone on this spread that you don't think is right, you come to me and ask about it. I'll either explain it to you or change it. But don't you be afraid to ask." The men nodded and went back to the corral to get their mounts, and Culbertson went back to the ranch house, where he found his foreman waiting for him. He motioned for Curly to follow him and went in the house to his office.

"Take a seat, Curly," Culbertson said. "What the hell

is going on? What's this business about the Johnson ranch and the herd up in the high pasture? You know damned well that I don't go in for that kind of crap."

Curly squirmed in his chair. "I'm sorry, boss. We'd been in town and had a few. Then when I heard that old man Johnson was dead, I thought that if we pestered the daughter, she might be more willing to sell out to you. We had a few more drinks and then went and raised a fuss at her ranch. I knew you wouldn't like it, but I guess the liquor got the best of me, and I wasn't thinking straight."

"You weren't thinking at all," Culbertson said. "And how about this business of Johnson being dead? That seems mighty convenient. You winning the ranch in a poker game and him getting murdered right after. You have something to do with that too?"

"Hell, no!" Curly replied. "That damned fool thought he had a winning hand, but he didn't have the money to call. So he reached into his pocket and pulled out this piece of paper, said it was the deed to his ranch. He signed it, threw it into the pot, and said 'call and raise.' But his full house wasn't as good as my straight flush. Ask Sheriff Gordon if you want. He was there and saw the whole thing."

"I might just do that, Curly." Culbertson started searching through the drawers in his desk. Finally, he pulled out a piece of paper from the bottom drawer. He picked up another document from the top of his desk and stared at both pieces carefully. Curly recognized the second piece as the deed to the Johnson place. The rancher's eyes narrowed and his face hardened. "Damn it all, you're lying to me, Curly. Look at that!" And he tossed a piece of paper across the desk toward his foreman. "That's a bill of sale I got from Johnson a couple of years ago when I bought that old wagon of his to turn into a chuck wagon for the trail drive. That signature isn't even close to the one on this phony deed you gave me. You're through here! Pack up your gear and get out."

Culbertson pulled a metal box from a drawer in his desk. He took a key from his vest pocket and unlocked it. Then he counted out some bills and handed them to Curly. "That's what you're due, plus an extra month's wages. You were a damned good foreman, but you don't work here anymore. I'm even beginning to believe that you had a hand in Henry Johnson's murder. I'm going to ride over to see Maria Johnson to apologize for your actions, and then I'm going to town and tell the sheriff what I know and what I suspect. You have that much of a head start. I wouldn't waste any time if I were you."

Curly leaped to his feet, kicking his chair over. "You can't do this to me!"

Culbertson stood, a Colt already in his hand and pointed at the foreman. "I already have. Now take a horse and be out of here in five minutes or I'll hog-tie you and take you into town myself."

Curly turned and headed for the door. "This ain't over. Not by a long shot," he said as he slammed out the door. Culbertson slumped back into his chair. His hand was shaking, not from fear but from anger. He would give

Curly more than five minutes, but not much more. *Damn it to hell. It's my fault. It's all my fault.*

Curly was in the bunkhouse, grumbling and slamming his things into his bedroll. "After all this time he just ups and fires me," he muttered to himself. "Well, we'll see who fires who. We're just going to have to move things up a little." Just then, Buster came in.

"Hey, Curly, what's going on?"

"Culbertson just fired me. I want you to get ahold of Sam, and the two of you meet me in town tonight."

"Fired you, huh?" Buster said. "You think he's wise to what's happening? You want we should ask for our pay and quit?"

"I don't give a damn what you do," Curly snarled. "But if I was you, I'd draw my pay while Culbertson's still alive to pay you." Curly snatched up his bedroll and saddlebags and headed for the barn.

Culbertson stepped out onto the porch. Billy was sitting on the bottom step. "I'm sorry, Mr. C., but I couldn't help overhearing some of what was said inside. Is there anything you want me to do?"

They both looked toward the barn as Curly came spurring out on his mount like both were on fire. Culbertson turned and saw Buster and Sam heading toward him. "Looks like we'll be needing to hire some new hands," he said, more to himself than anyone else. "Yes, there is, Billy. You can saddle Juniper for me and bring him up. You might saddle a horse for yourself too. We have some fences to mend, and we'll need to hire some help. As of now, I'm making you top hand. Whether or not you keep the job will be up to you. You think you can handle it?"

"Me, top hand! Yes, sir, I think I can do the job. Don't worry. I won't let you down, Mr. Culbertson. I know I've got some to learn, but I can do it. If I should let you down, it won't be for lack of tryin'," Billy said as he hurried off to the barn.

Culbertson watched him go and said to himself, "I know it won't, son. I know it won't." Then, turning back toward the two hands as they walked up, Culbertson said, "Wait right here, men. I'll get your pay."

Chapter Twelve

Maria took one last whisk with the broom at the edge of the porch, whirled around, and entered the house, closing the door behind her. She set the broom next to the door and moved to the stove, picked up the coffeepot, emptied the contents into the sink, and pumped fresh water into the pot. As she prepared the coffee, she spoke over her shoulder to Earl. "There's no need to sit there by the corner of the window like a bump on a log. You can move over to the table and be more comfortable. You can still see out the window from there, and no one will see you."

"Matt told me to keep an eye out for trouble, and I intend to do just that."

Maria placed the pot on the stove and turned to him, drying her hands on her apron. "You silly goose." She laughed. "He didn't mean you couldn't move. You can be sociable and still keep watch."

Earl got up, leaned the scattergun next to the window, and took a seat at the table, turning his chair so he had a better view out the window. Maria sat down across from him. They sat there for a few moments in silence that was finally broken by the young deputy.

"What're you going to do now?" he asked. "I mean, I know you haven't had much time to think about it, but running a ranch is a considerable chore. You're going to need help."

"You're right; I haven't had time to think about it. So much has happened so quickly," Maria said with a noticeable quiver in her voice. "Mama and Daddy are buried on the hill out back, and I've already told Mr. Culbertson that I intend to be here for a good long while. But I don't have any clear idea as to how I'm going to be able to do all that needs doing."

Earl cleared his throat and said, "Well, I'll help you in any way I can. I'll even stop being a deputy, if I *am* still a deputy, and go to work for you full time if that's what it takes. I've been courting you for some time now, Maria, and I know that now is not the time to bring that up, but I really do care for you, and I'll wait and work and help you keep this place going until you tell me not to."

Maria sat silently for a few minutes. Then she got up and went to the stove and poured two cups of coffee. She moved back to the table, set one of the cups in front of Earl, and then resumed her place. She sipped from her cup and then said quietly, "You're sweet, Earl, and I am attracted to you, but before you were always working for the sheriff and doing what was best for Mr. Culbertson and the Circle C. I was never certain that you could be trusted. Now I'm beginning to see things a little differently." She reached across the table and took his hand.

Earl looked into her eyes for a long moment and then reached over and gently stroked her cheek. "Maria, I . . . uh . . . ," he stammered. Before he could finish, he caught a movement out of the corner of his eye. "Someone's coming," he said as he jumped up and moved to his place beside the window, picking up the shotgun.

Maria looked out the window at the rider who was approaching the house. "I don't recognize him. Earl, don't jump to any conclusions. We don't know if he's from the Circle C or not. I'll go out and see what he wants."

"Be careful, Maria. Don't take any chances and don't get in my line of fire."

Maria set her Winchester just inside the door, opened it, and stepped into the doorway. The rider crossed the little creek and rode into the yard. He touched his hat by way of respect and said, "Afternoon, ma'am. Would you be Miss Maria Johnson?"

"Yes, I would."

"I heard what happened to your father, ma'am. Please accept my condolences."

"Thank you kindly. What can I do for you?"

"Well, ma'am, I'm U.S. Marshal Jacob Bearson, and I was told that I might find a man by the name of Matthew Stoker here."

Maria's heart skipped a beat, but she remained calm on the outside. "I'm sorry, Marshal, but there's no one here by that name."

Marshal Bearson took off his hat, pulled his bandanna from around his neck, and wiped some of the dust and sweat from his weathered face. His hair was black and hung down to his shoulders. He wore neither beard nor mustache. His eyes were as black as coal, and when they looked at Maria, it was as if they pierced right through to her inner self.

"Miss Johnson," he said, "we could sit here and beat around the bush for a while, but we'd pretty much wind up going where I intend to go anyway. I suspect that Matthew's not here at the moment, 'cause you don't seem the kind of woman that would tell an out-and-out lie, but I also suspect that you know where he is. Besides, if we fool around here much longer, that jasper behind the curtain might get a bit antsy, and I'd have to shoot him. Now, that wouldn't please me much or him at all. I know Matthew, and I'm not here to take him in, but I do need to talk with him."

"I'm sorry, Marshal. You're right, of course," Maria said. "The last two days have been unsettling, to say the least. Mr. Stoker is on his way to the Culbertson ranch. Marshal, I just made a fresh pot of coffee. Won't you come in and have some? I'll tell you what I can."

"I never turn down a cup of coffee." Marshal Bearson smiled. "Especially when it's offered by a pretty young woman."

As he swung down from his buckskin, Maria noticed he was a lean and hard man. About six feet tall and 180 pounds, he moved with the same catlike grace she had observed in Matthew Stoker. She suspected they were two of a kind and that this man would not be a person one should underestimate. He moved almost lackadaisically, but she noticed that nothing escaped his eye; he was alert to all about him. He stretched his left arm and swung it around in an arc as if trying to loosen it up. As he walked to the porch and up the steps, Maria noticed that he had a slight limp. He started to slap the dust from his clothes with his hat and then stopped. He went back down the steps and finished the job on the ground.

"Sorry, ma'am. My wife used to sweep the porch first thing every morning. She'd give me the dickens if I brushed the dust from the trail off my clothes and onto the porch."

"Does your wife live in these parts?" Maria asked.

"No, ma'am, she died several years ago—both she and my daughter—but still a day doesn't go by that I don't think about the two of them."

"I'm sorry, Marshal Bearson. And it's not ma'am. It's Maria. Please come in."

"Name's Jacob, and thank you, Maria. After you."

They walked into the house, and Maria headed for the stove. Earl was standing in the corner, with the shotgun pointed at the marshal. Jacob reached over and hung his hat on a peg on the wall. He turned back toward Earl and said, "If you're going to shoot me, son, I would appreciate it if you'd wait till I've had a cup of coffee. It smells awfully good."

Maria poured a cup and set it on the table. "Marshal, this is Earl Burns," she said. "Earl, stop pointing that shotgun at the marshal."

Jacob sat down, took a healthy whiff, smiled, and took a sip. "You know, son, if you keep watch from here in the middle of the room, you get a much wider view and during the daylight no one can see you like I did when you were peeking around the curtain."

Earl leaned the scattergun against the windowsill and started toward the table. "No, no, son!" the marshal said. "Never leave your weapon where you can't reach it. You never know when you'll need it. There are lots of ways to approach this house that can't be seen through the window. Always think the best, but prepare for the worst. This is mighty fine coffee, Miss Maria. Just a touch of chicory. That's the way my Songbird used to make it."

"Was she a good cook?" Maria asked as she took a seat at the table.

"Yes, ma'am, she was, but not the kind of food you're thinking of. Indian food. She was a full-blooded Comanche and fixed food the way her mama taught her. But she learned to fix coffee with chicory after she heard me raving about Matthew's." Jacob paused and listened a minute. "Rider coming from the north."

Earl grabbed the shotgun and got up and went to the door. He opened it and stepped out onto the porch and then stuck his head in and said, "It's all right. It's just Clay."

"Clay?" the marshal asked.

"Clay Harper," Maria replied. "He came out with Earl to bring Daddy home and has been staying on to lend a hand."

"Clay Harper. Hmm. Seems I recall the sheriff saying something about him. Said he was 'in cahoots' with Matthew."

"He and Mr. Stoker were together when they found Daddy's body, but I don't think they knew each other before that day."

The door opened and Earl came in, followed by Clay. "Clay, this here is marshal Jacob Bearson," Earl said. "Marshal, Clay Harper."

"Howdy, Mr. Harper," Jacob said, extending his hand. "We were just talking about you," he said as they shook.

"Oh?" Clay responded. "Have I done something to arouse the curiosity of the law?"

"The marshal was just telling me that the sheriff thinks you and Matthew are in cahoots. Isn't that what you said?" Maria asked.

"Well," Jacob answered, "that's what the sheriff said. He went on to say that he wouldn't be surprised if Matthew and Clay hadn't killed your daddy."

"That's ridiculous," she said. "Why, Mr. Stoker went into town to find my father and tell him that I wanted him to come home. From what I've heard, my father was dead long before Matthew ever even got to Twin Forks."

Clay nodded in agreement and added, "If Matthew had been around town before he came to the livery stable, I would've known about it. Folks tend to take little notice of me. In fact, I heard some of Culbertson's men talking about a gunslinger who was new to the area when they came in to put their horses up. They were wondering how the Johnsons came to know him and whether or not he'd be coming into town."

"Besides," Earl chimed in, "Matt would never shoot a

man in the back. He wouldn't have to. Especially with Maria's father. He was no hand with a gun."

Jacob put his hands up. "Okay, okay, I didn't put much stock in the sheriff's theory, but you're wrong, son. Matthew would and has shot a man in the back. I know that for a fact." He paused and then said very quietly, "Yes, sir, I surely do."

Jacob sat quietly for a long time while the others kept staring at him. "I'm not sure that I should tell you about it, but he never told me not to, and it would certainly tell you a lot about the man called Matthew Stoker."

"Well, if it's something bad about Mr. Stoker, I, for one, don't want to know," Maria said. "No matter what he's done in the past, he has been a gentleman here, and in my case, probably a lifesaver."

The marshal raised his eyebrows. "Oh? What happened?" he asked. Maria told him of the events of the preceding day. After listening to her story, Jacob said, "That sounds like Matthew. I'm terribly sorry for your ordeal, Maria. If you pour me another cup of coffee, I'll tell you my story, and from my point of view, nothing in it puts Matthew in a negative light. No, ma'am, nothing at all."

Maria got up, plucked the pot from the stove, and filled the marshal's cup and the cups of the others. Finally, she filled her own and then set the pot in the middle of the table. "Just help yourself to as much as you want. I can always make more," she said.

"Let's see. It was thirteen—no, fourteen years ago. I had only been on the job for three months," Jacob said.

"The main office had sent me out to get Jeb Preston. I was following the tracks of Preston's gang. I came around a rocky outcrop, and there were five men pointing pistols at me."

"Good heavens!" Maria exclaimed. "What did you do?"

"The only thing I could think of. I told them that they were all under arrest," Jacob said. "The whole gang laughed at that. Then Jeb said that he had never shot a U.S. marshal until now. It was then that I noticed a rider on the ridge behind Preston. Later I found out that it was Matthew. Anyway, I saw Jeb pull back the hammer on his pistol, and then he lurched forward as he pulled the trigger. The bullet hit me in the thigh. I dove out of the saddle and grabbed my Colt from the holster. As I did so, I felt a pain in my shoulder. I got off a shot at one of the gang who was aiming at me and hit him in the chest. As I hit the ground, I heard a rifle shot and the sound of two riders running off. Then I passed out." Jacob took a large swallow from his cup.

"It sounds like you were lucky you didn't die," Clay commented.

"What happened then?" Earl asked.

Jacob finished his coffee and pushed the cup toward the pot. "I have no idea," he said. "When I woke up, I was lying on my blankets, all bandaged up. I looked around and saw a man sitting with his back against a tree, reading a book. I tried to get up but fell back. He came over to me, told me his name, and said that it would be a while before I'd be up and around. I asked if he was a doctor, and he told me no but that he'd been studying to be one.

He also said that he got a lot of practice dealing with gunshot wounds during the war. Later, when we were talking, he told me that he had graduated from Harvard back in Massachusetts. When I was able to ride, we came to the town of Hugoton, and he told me to have a doctor look at my wounds. I asked if he was coming with me, and he told me that it wouldn't look good if a deputy U.S. marshal was seen in the company of a known gunfighter. Well, I saw the doctor, and he told me that he couldn't have done better than Matthew."

Chapter Thirteen

Matthew and I have seen each other a number of times since then, sometimes by accident, sometimes on purpose. So, you see," Jacob said, pouring himself another cup of coffee, "I know for a fact that Matthew Stoker has shot at least two men in the back, and I am damned glad that he did. Excuse my language, ma'am."

"But that's different," Clay said. "He was saving a deputy marshal's life."

"Maybe so, but how could he be certain that I was the law and they weren't?"

"You mean you had never met him before?" Maria asked.

Jacob shook his head. "Nope. I don't know; he may have seen me around, but not so I would know it. Afterward I learned about his reputation—that most thought he was very fast on the draw—which I'd already pretty much figured out on my own."

"I guarantee you he is one of the fastest around," Clay

said. "I saw him draw against young Billy Bronson, and it was only a blur."

"Oh? What happened?" Jacob asked.

"Nothing much," Clay replied. "I figure Billy had been drinking pretty heavily when Matthew went into the Lucky Lady. He tried to force Matthew to draw, but Stoker ignored him. Finally, Billy went too far, and Matthew faced him. Billy made the first move, but before his gun was half-way out of the leather, he was staring down the barrel of Matthew's Colt. Billy just froze, and Matthew took his gun away and went back to sipping his beer."

"Humph!" Jacob snorted. "Matthew must be getting old. He always said never draw unless you mean to shoot, and then shoot to kill. 'Draw fast, shoot straight, and put it away slow.' Those were his words. Hey, thank you for the coffee, Miss Johnson. I'd better be getting on my way. You said that Matthew was heading for the Culbertson spread?"

"That's right, Marshal. It's a pretty fair ride from here," she replied.

"I know," Jacob said, getting up and putting on his hat. "I've been there on a couple of occasions. If I miss him and he comes back here, tell him to wait here for me. There's something going on, that's for sure. And I aim to get to the bottom of it." He turned, went out the door and down the steps, and swung up into his saddle. Clay, Earl, and Maria had followed him out onto the porch. Jacob tipped his hat to Maria and focused a minute on the other two. "Why were you watching from behind the curtain, son?" he asked.

"Matt said it might be a good idea to keep out of sight. A bunch of riders came in shouting and firing into the air last night, and if they came back, Matt thought it would be better if they were surprised to find someone here other than Maria."

"Good idea," the marshal said. "Better keep it that way until we find out what's really going on around here." He touched the brim of his hat again. "Ma'am," he said and turned his horse and rode out.

As the three of them watched the marshal go, Earl said, "There goes one man I wouldn't want to get on the wrong side of."

"Uh-huh," Clay said. "He and Matthew are cut from the same cloth. It wouldn't be very wise for anyone to cross either of them."

Maria turned and headed into the house. "As long as you two are going to be hiding inside, you might as well give me a hand with the dishes and the housecleaning."

"Hiding! We ain't hiding. We're just doing what Matt told us to do," Earl said defensively.

"Sure you are, Earl," she said with a wink toward Clay. "But don't worry, I'll protect you if any big, bad men come riding in."

Earl went in after her, protesting that he wasn't afraid and that dishes and housecleaning were not proper chores for a deputy sheriff. Clay shook his head, smiled, followed them in, and shut the door.

Chapter Fourteen

Damn it, Curly, how could you be so stupid? Didn't you know that Culbertson had a copy of Johnson's signature?" Sheriff Gordon had been carrying on for several minutes. Curly stood there taking it in with a half smirk on his face. "Things were going just dandy. Nobody suspected a thing, but now you get fired and Culbertson's coming to town to tell me you were involved in Johnson's murder."

"Relax, Gordon," Curly said. "Things have just started to move a little faster, is all."

Just then the door to the sheriff's office swung open, and Sam and Buster walked in.

"You guys draw your pay?" Curly asked, and both men nodded.

"That means no one is left on the Circle C to let us know what's happening out there. Jesus, Curly, what the hell is going on?" Gordon screamed.

"Simmer down, Bob. I've got a plan," Curly said. "Culbertson's going to see the Johnson girl before he comes into town. Sam and Buster and I will get there ahead of him and drop him as he rides in. Then we'll ride into town and say the gunfighter shot Culbertson, and you can raise a posse and see to it that they bring him in dead. After that, it'll be easy to handle the girl, and we'll have a clear shot at the final two parcels of land that the railroad will need. Culbertson once told me that he had no kin. So it should be easy for you to pick up the Circle C for taxes."

The sheriff considered the idea and finally mused, "It just might work. Once the gunslinger is dead, we can blame Johnson's death on him too. Of course, we'll have to kill Harper too. I haven't seen him around lately, but I'm bettin' he's with the gunfighter. Won't be any great loss. Even though I can't believe anyone would pay him any mind, you might as well kill him anyway."

"You're right," Curly said. "He could be a problem. If he's out at the Johnson place, we had better say that he and the gunfighter both opened up on Culbertson. Then you and the posse can bring them both in. But I wouldn't underestimate him."

"Oh, hell," the sheriff said. "I never seen a one of them that was worth the sweat off my holster. You three better get moving and try not to mess things up this time. I'll go down to the Lucky Lady and pour a little courage into some of the boys that would do well in a posse."

"Right. Come on, fellas. Let's see what we can stir up at the Johnson place," Curly said and headed out the door. Sam and Buster trailed along behind.

Chapter Fifteen

Y̱ou know, Drella, this is mighty pretty country." Matt had pulled up at the top of a small rise. A stream wound its way across the valley to the right of him, and the mountains rose in the distance ahead. The valley and hills were lush and green. "I hope the place we're heading for is as rich and fertile as this land. No wonder Johnson pulled off here to settle, huh, big girl?"

The dog just sat there, looking out over the valley. Suddenly she stood, the hair on the nape of her neck standing up, her nose sniffing the air. Matt straightened in the saddle and looked in the direction that Drella was staring. Then Drella's hair fell back in place and her tail started to wag. Matt watched as a rider rode up out of a gully about a half mile away. "I do wish I had your ears and your sense of smell, girl. I'm going to head down to that stream and get some coffee going. You go ahead and show him the way. Go on!"

Drella took off like a shot, and Matt watched her as she raced toward the horseman. When she was a couple hundred yards away, the rider dismounted and squatted on his heels with his arms open wide. Drella barreled into him like an out-of-control freight train, knocking him over, and the two of them rolled around on the ground like a couple of kids. Matt got to the stream and fished in his saddlebags for his coffee and a pot. He gathered some kindling and small pieces of wood. He found a reasonably flat rock and built a fire around it. Then he waded out in the stream for clearer water and filled the pot. He dropped in some coffee, added a little chicory, and placed the pot on the rock. By the time Drella and the marshal arrived, the coffee was well under way.

"I thought you two had gone off and left me to drink this coffee by myself," Matt said.

"Well, I tried to talk her into it, but she said that it wouldn't be right to go off without saying good-bye," Jacob said. "How the hell have you been, Matthew?" Jacob asked, slapping Matt on the back. "I haven't run into you two in more than a year."

The two men shook hands, and Matt said, "We've been doing fine until the last couple of days. What about you? I hear you brought in Ed Lowery and his bunch a while back."

Jacob smiled. "Yeah, they gave me two whole days off for bringing in that bunch, but it's the last couple of days that I want to talk to you about."

"Time enough for that after we have some coffee. I see you're still riding the buckskin."

Jacob reached into his saddlebag and pulled out a cup. "Old Mischief has the best single-foot walk I ever sat astride. She's got a few more good years in her, but I'll have to start looking for a replacement soon. She doesn't deserve to be driven into the ground. I see you're riding the filly. She wasn't much more than two years old when I saw you last. Damnedest thing I ever saw, her and Drella following you around wherever you went. Whatever happened to your old mount? What was her name? Athena, that was it. You and your book-learned names! This one's Aphrodite, isn't she?"

Matt chuckled. "That's right. I turned Athena out with a wild bunch I ran across up in the Dakotas. It seemed to me that she deserved to have a little fun after putting up with me all those years."

"True enough," Jacob said. "You do lead a life that would wear out anyone, man or beast."

"I'm thinking of changing that," Matt told him. "I think it's time to hang up my gun and settle down, Jacob."

"Well, all I can say, Matthew, is it's about time. Damn it, man! I can't think of anything you could've said that would make me happier." The two men sat, drinking coffee and catching up on the past several months. Finally, Jacob said, "All this is well and good, but I need to know what's been going on around here. The local sheriff says you killed a man, shot him in the back. Now, I don't believe that for one minute, but something's going on and you're smack-dab in the middle of it."

"I wish I knew, Jacob," Matt said. "I'm as confused as you are. As far as the sheriff's concerned, I think I'm just a convenient target. But there's something rotten in the state of Nebraska, to paraphrase one of my favorite authors.

All I did was ride into a ranch and ask for a chance to water my stock and wash up."

Matt related the events of the past few days. When he was through, he added, "I tell you, Jacob, it just doesn't add up. When I was talking with Culbertson just a little while ago, he didn't say much, but I could tell from his eyes that a lot of what I was saying was coming as a surprise to the man. I had him pegged for the villain in the piece, but now I don't think so."

"I've met Culbertson," Jacob said. "He's ambitious and maybe a little greedy, but all in all, I think he's an honest man."

Matt thought for a minute as he rolled a smoke and lit it. "You don't suppose that some of the hands are doing this on their own, do you?"

"Maybe," Jacob replied, "but it seems unlikely. I think there's another player in the game."

"But to what end?" Matt asked. "Culbertson's the only one who stands to benefit. Maybe some relative is trying to horn in on him."

"Culbertson's told me he doesn't have any relatives that he's aware of," Jacob said. "He's told me that he had concerns about what would happen to the Circle C if he had an accident and died. He was even thinking of going east to try to find a woman who would marry him and give him an heir."

"There must be something else that would explain all that's happening here, but damned if I've come across it in the short time I've been here," Matt muttered, half to himself.

"There is," Jacob said, "but the information has only gone out to a select few in order to keep things from getting out of hand. The railroad is putting through a spur to serve the cattlemen on the western end of the state. They've tried very hard to keep the news quiet for fear of land speculators trying to make a profit at the expense of both those who own the land that the railroad will travel through and the railroad itself."

"How did you come by that information?" Matt asked.

"The Commissioner of Indian Affairs informed the U.S. marshals of the area so that we could protect the rights of the Indians and see to it that if their lands were to be used, the benefits would go to the tribes. I just came back from talking with chiefs from the Sioux and Arapaho tribes."

"You know," Matt said, "if politicians are involved, there's no such thing as a secret. Do you know of anyone else in Twin Forks who might have the contacts who could supply that kind of information?"

"Not really. Maybe a banker. They always seem to have influential connections, but I think a banker in Twin Forks would be pretty small potatoes. Hell, I don't even know if there is a banker in that town."

Matt shook his head. "The whole damn thing is like a Greek play. I guess we'll have to wait for the messenger bringing good news before we can unravel this mess."

"You know I don't know anything about Greek plays, Matthew. But whatever's going on, I'm going to get to the bottom of it. Enough about that. Let's have another cup of coffee."

Chapter Sixteen

I never knew what was going on, Billy," Culbertson said, "and that's the God's honest truth."

"I believe you, Mr. Culbertson. Not many at the Circle C did. We knew that Curly and the others were making trouble for some of the homesteaders, but we thought they were doing it on your orders. After all, you did buy the Grogan place after he and his family pulled up stakes. We figured the others was just the same."

Culbertson reined up and looked out over the valley. He could make out the Johnson place at the far western end. "I bought the Grogan spread after he came to me and said that he wasn't cut out for this kind of life. I gave him a good price, and he told me that he was going to go back to running a general store once he found a place that needed one or had one for sale. He told me that he had been a storekeeper back in Illinois before he came out here. I didn't need his land, but I felt sorry for his wife and youngsters."

"All I know," Billy said, "is shortly after that, Curly told us you wanted all them that was settling on land next to the Circle C driven off. I only went with them one time, and I didn't care much for the way they was doing things, like killing livestock and spoiling wells. After that, I always found something else to do. I've even been thinking of moving on and looking for work elsewhere."

Culbertson looked at the young man carefully, as if for the first time. "How old are you, Billy?"

"Twenty-three, sir."

"How much schooling have you had? Can you read and write?"

"Yes, sir, pretty good. I went to school until I was thirteen. My ma always said that the only way to make something of yourself was to get an education."

"Very good advice. Where are your parents now?"

Billy looked down and started toying with the reins. "My ma and pa are both dead." He hesitated for a moment and then went on. "They was killed by a bunch of renegades. They hit our place while I was at school. When I got home, the place was burned to the ground, and they was laying in the yard. It looked as if them that done it had their way with my ma before they killed her." Tears were sliding down his cheeks. "I buried them and put a halter on an old swayback nag that we had. The only animal left." His face broke into a slight smile. "Horse wasn't good for nothing, but my ma wouldn't let her be put down. She used to say, 'That horse gave us the best she had to give, and she has a right to live out the rest of her days naturally.' Anyway, I just climbed onto old Nancy and never looked back. After a few days, I came to the Bar K and rode right in with all the hands snickering at me and Nancy and asked for a job. They took me on. After a few years, I'd made enough to have my own horse and outfit. Then, with a little money in my pocket, I set out to see the country, hoping to find a place where I could make my mark, working here and there whenever I could. Finally, five years ago, I rode in to the Circle C."

"Don't you have any kin anywhere?"

"Not that I know of. Ma and Pa never spoke of none."

"Well, damned if you and I aren't a pair," Culbertson said. "I don't have any relatives either. And here I am building the biggest ranch in the territory without a soul to turn it over to when my days are done. Humph! Well, that's a problem for another day. Who taught you to use a Colt?"

"My pa taught me to shoot, and a hand at the Bar K showed me how to use a pistol. I practiced with him every day until I got nearly as good as him. He was good, but one day he met a man who was better. I learned then not to make much of a show about it unless you were ready to die. I don't know what got into me the other day. Too much drink, I guess. I'm sorry that I made such a fool of myself, Mr. Culbertson."

"Billy, I'm just glad you were smart enough and sober enough to know when to give it up. Listen, Billy, you think you're good enough to take on the job of ramrodding the Circle C? You'll have to quit sowing your wild oats, and you'll have to hone up on your reading and writing skills. The other hands may not like a younger fellow giving the orders, so you may have to prove yourself to some of them, but I don't want it done by fighting unless there's no other way. What do you say?"

"I think I can do the job, Mr. Culbertson. Leastways I'll give you the best that I got. And except when I'm being a fool, I have never believed that fighting solves a problem, and I promise you my foolish days are over. If I'm wrong, you won't have to let me go. I'll leave on my own."

"It's settled then. I'll tell the other hands when we get back. Of course, I still have to come up with a foreman, and I don't think there is anyone on the ranch that can handle that job. I'll probably have to put the word out around the region to find a man capable of taking charge. Let's get over to the Johnson place and then into town to see the sheriff. We have a lot to take care of."

Both men kicked their horses up to a land-eating trot and headed across the valley floor.

Chapter Seventeen

Curly, Buster, and Sam rode into a stand of sycamores about a hundred yards away from the Johnson house. They dismounted, drew their carbines from their scabbards, and moved quietly to the edge of the trees.

"Look yonder," Curly said. "That looks like that big black stallion of Culbertson's coming now, and if I don't miss my guess, that's Billy Bronson's pinto coming with him. They're still about twenty minutes out. Pick your places and aim careful. It's Culbertson we want, but if Billy gets in the way and goes down, so be it."

The three picked spots where they could cover the front yard of the Johnson place. "Let 'em get close to the house. Make it easier to say they was shot by those inside," Curly ordered.

Inside the house, Maria, Clay, and Earl were watching the approach of the two riders. "It looks like Mr. Culbertson and Billy Bronson," Earl said. "I don't see any others."

"Yeah," Clay said. "Doesn't look like trouble, but stay alert just the same until we know what they want."

"Looks pretty quiet," Culbertson said as they approached the front yard.

"Maybe no one's home," Billy said.

"Hello, Maria, are you there?"

Clay motioned Maria toward the door. She was just pulling it open when a shot rang out. Earl rushed and shoved her out of the way, slamming the door at the same time. More shots rang out.

"What the hell!" Clay shouted. "Those shots are coming from the left." He pushed open the shutters on that side of the house, saw gun smoke coming from the trees, and opened fire. Earl rushed over and joined in, shooting at the sounds coming from the tree line.

The conversation by the stream was interrupted when Drella got to her feet and a low rumble came from her throat. The two men looked around and saw nothing. Then the sound of gunfire reached them. "That's coming from the Johnson place," Matt said as he poured the remainder of the coffee on the fire and threw the pot and his cup into his saddlebags. Jacob was right behind him, and they both swung into their saddles simultaneously. Drella was already off and running, the two men urging their horses after her.

As Culbertson hollered out his greeting, Billy heard a gunshot and saw Culbertson start to fall from the saddle. He lunged from the saddle across Culbertson's mount, grabbing him by the shoulders and shielding Culbertson with his body. As they fell to the ground, he felt Culbertson's body jerk from another impact and felt a searing pain in his own shoulder. He fumbled to get his pistol out while keeping on top of Culbertson.

"There's more than one person in the house, and I can see two riders coming hell-bent for leather," Curly said. "Let's get out of here. We done what we come for." The three of them headed for their horses.

Billy had gotten his Colt out and fired at the movement in the woods. He had the satisfaction of hearing a yelp from one of the bushwhackers. He didn't go after them, turning his attention instead to Culbertson. "I need help!" he cried to the house. "Mr. Culbertson's been hurt bad."

Maria started out the door, but Earl grabbed hold of her. "You can't go out there. They might be waiting for some-one to come bolting out to help."

"Earl, the shooting has stopped. If they were still out there, they would have shot Billy. I've got to go. He needs help."

"Well, let me go first. It still might be a trap."

Earl led the way, with Maria following. Clay came out onto the porch and kept his eyes on the trees where the shots had come from. Maria knelt down beside Billy and Culbertson. "He's alive, but he's been shot twice, and he's lost a lot of blood," she said.

With Drella leading the way, the marshal and Matt rode in and dismounted. They took in the situation at a glance. "Is anyone else hurt?" Matt asked.

"I took one in the shoulder," Billy said, "but Mr. Culbertson's the one who needs help."

"Right. Jacob, give me a hand, and we'll move him into the house. Earl, you and Maria clear off the table. We'll lay him out there. Clay, you tend to the horses and bring in my saddlebags. I'm going to need them. Billy, you just take it easy. We'll take a look at your shoulder after we've attended to Culbertson."

Matt and the marshal carefully picked up Culbertson, carried him into the house, and placed him on the table. Clay came in, carrying Matt's saddlebags. "Good, give them to me. Maria, get some water boiling." Matt fished into his saddlebags and came out with a cloth-bound packet. "Maria, when the water's boiling, drop these instruments in. Now, let's see what we have here."

Matt turned to the table and looked at Culbertson. He slipped his hunting knife from his boot and carefully cut away Culbertson's shirt and the upper half of his long johns. "I need a clean, wet cloth."

Maria took several from the cupboard and dropped them in the not-yet-boiling water, wrung them out, and handed them to Matt. He cleaned the wounds as thoroughly as he could and examined them. "It looks like the one that hit him in the side bounced off a rib or two and exited just below the breastplate. I don't think there was any damage to his organs, maybe a cracked or broken rib or two is all, so we'll just bandage it up and turn him over and look at the one that's just below the shoulder. The bullet is still in there, and it may have done more damage." He wadded up some of the clean cloths, placed them over the entrance and exit wounds, and secured them with long strips of cloth wrapped around the rancher's body and tied tightly. Then, with Jacob's help, he carefully turned Culbertson over to examine the other wound.

Matt got a clean towel and spread it out on the table. He turned to Maria and said, "Once the instruments have been boiling for about five minutes, dump the water out and then, using a clean cloth, place them on this towel."

While he waited, he took a look at Billy's shoulder. "You are a lucky young man. The bullet just went through flesh. It didn't hit bone or muscle. Of course, you probably wish it had missed you altogether, but you can't have everything."

"Is Mr. Culbertson going to be all right?"

"I don't know, but we'll do what we can and then wait and see. Let me get a bandage on this shoulder, and you should keep your arm in a sling for a few days."

Jacob spoke up. "What the hell went on here, anyway?"

"We were just riding in to apologize to Miss Maria for the trouble the hands have been causing when someone started shooting at us from the trees, yonder," Billy replied.

Clay said, "When I heard the shots, I glanced out the window and saw this young fellow throw himself on Culbertson's back while he was falling from the saddle. More 'an likely, the shot that hit him would be in Culbertson now if he hadn't done that. Probably kept Culbertson alive."

"Couldn't get a look at any of them," Earl chimed in, "but I think there was at least three of them." The others nodded in agreement with his assessment.

"I think I might have winged one of them," Billy said. "I got off a shot and heard one of them yelp."

"I'll get on their tracks after we're done here," Jacob said. "Shouldn't be too hard to follow. Ain't that many places for them to go."

"Everything's ready, Matthew," Maria said.

"Thank you, Maria. Let's get to it, then," Matt said. He went to the table, picked up an instrument, and carefully probed where the bullet had entered. "There it is," he said. "If my memory's correct, it's lodged right near both the kidney and the lung. The trick now is to get the bullet out without damaging either organ. It's tricky work, but I'm willing to try, or I could leave it in until we can get him to a proper doctor."

"The only person in town who does any doctoring is the barber," Earl said. "He's good for scrapes and bruises, but I don't think he has much experience with taking out bullets."

"You can do it, Matthew," Jacob said. "I know that for a fact. I believe Culbertson couldn't be in better hands."

"What do you think, son?" Matt asked Billy. "You're the nearest thing to kin he has here."

"I think Mr. Culbertson would want you to do what you think is best, Mr. Stoker, and I believe what's best is you doing what you can for him."

"All right, son, I'll do the best I can. Jacob, you and Clay hold him down. Even though he's unconscious, his body will react to pain, and I'll be working close enough to vital organs that any movement on his part could wind up finishing what the bad guys started."

Matt picked up another instrument that looked like a long, skinny, fragile pair of pliers. It took about fifteen minutes of intense work, but finally, he held up the slug for all to see. His face was covered with sweat when he dropped the slug onto the towel. He crossed to his saddle-bags and pulled out another packet, from which he took out some thread and a needle.

"What are you going to do with that?" Earl asked.

"I'm going to sew up the wounds. I'll leave a small opening in each so they can drain. It will keep the wounds cleaner, help prevent infection, and leave a smaller scar. After I'm through with Culbertson, you'll be next, Billy. Maria, get me some of that brandy you gave us. I'll use it to keep bacteria out of the wounds."

Nearly an hour later, Matt stepped back and sank down in a chair. "I truly enjoy your coffee, Maria, but if you happen to have anything stronger, I could sure use it about now. I've used up all the brandy."

Maria got up and went to a cupboard. "Daddy always kept a bottle for what he called 'the miseries.' I don't know how good it is, but from my father's reaction, it certainly is strong." She put the bottle and a cup in front of Matt. He poured a generous shot and tossed it off in a single move. He then poured another and passed the bottle to the others.

"Okay, let's talk about what happened," Matt said as he took another sip.

"All any of us know," Clay offered, "is that someone opened up on Culbertson and Billy as they rode up to the house. If I had to guess, I'd say they wanted to lay the blame at our doorstep."

"You're probably right," the marshal said. "But who and why, that's what we need to know, although Matthew and I have suspicions about the why."

"Mr. Culbertson ran Curly off the ranch earlier today," Billy said, "and a couple of other hands left right after. He didn't say, but I think it was because of some of the things you told him, Mr. Stoker. Curly is a cantankerous sort, and I believe he'd be capable of dry-gulching anyone he had a grudge against. But why here, I just don't know."

Jacob got up and headed for the door. "I'll go out and see if I can pick up their tracks. Matthew, you better stay here until I get back."

"Okay, Jacob, but you take care. I don't want a repeat of the Preston episode."

"Neither do I, but I've learned a lot since then. I'll just see what I can find out and then head back here, but I'd feel better knowing there was someone keeping an eye on things here."

Matt nodded in agreement. "You're right. Billy, you think you can ride?"

"Sure, what do you want me to do? Go with the marshal?"

"No, it's pretty clear that, whoever they were, they were trying to kill Culbertson. I want you to go to the Circle C and get a few men you can trust and bring them here. Don't tell them why, and don't tell them what has happened. Just say that Mr. Culbertson wants them. After you're well on your way back here, you can tell them what happened. If any say they want no part of it, let them go back. If it was Curly and his friends, there may still be supporters at the ranch. With everything else that's going on, we don't need to be watching our backs."

"I know just the men to pick. Don't any of them think much of Curly, and they all have a lot of respect for Mr. Culbertson." Billy followed the marshal out, and everyone in the house watched both men ride off.

"Let's move Culbertson to a more comfortable location," Matt said.

"You can put him in Daddy's room. I'll turn down the covers."

"You sit, Matthew," Clay said. "Earl and I will move him. I think you've done enough. Sit and enjoy your drink."

Chapter Eighteen

Matt sat at the table and took another sip of the whiskey. Drella got up from the corner where she had been watching everything, walked over to Matt, and laid her head in his lap. He smiled and scratched her gently behind the ear. "I don't know about you, big girl, but these last few days have been strange and hectic. Maybe you could ask your fairy godmother to wave her magic wand and set everything right."

The dog looked up at him with those big brown eyes and cocked her head in that quizzical manner that always made Matt smile.

"You really want to understand, don't you?" he laughed. "Sometimes I think you understand a whole lot more than I give you credit for. You've saved my hide on more than one occasion, and I am very grateful."

The others came out of the bedroom and took seats around the table. "He seems to be resting comfortably," Maria said. "Where did you ever learn so much about doctoring?"

"Some of it came from books, but mostly from the war. There were always a lot of bullet wounds and very few doctors. One thing about war—it teaches you how to do many things you never figured you'd be doing. Not only can I extract bullets, but I'm a pretty fair cook as well."

"Well, after what I saw here, I can tell you that if I ever get in the way of a bullet, I hope you're around," Earl said.

"Better to hope you're never in the way of a bullet," Clay said as he moved to a window. "Getting kind of dark out. I don't think the marshal's going to be able to follow the trail of those bushwhackers much longer."

"Jacob won't have any trouble," Matt said. "He's three-quarters Comanche. He could track a lizard in a sand-storm."

Maria got up and put the coffeepot on. "The marshal said that the two of you have known each other for some time."

"More than thirteen years. I was the equivalent of best man at his wedding and later was the equivalent of god-father to his daughter."

"Equivalent?" Clay asked.

"Jacob married a Comanche woman at their winter camp, and when his daughter was born, he asked me if I would become blood brother to the girl. Jacob, Song-bird, and Little Sparrow were the closest thing to family I've had since I left the East."

"Jacob told us that his wife and daughter were dead," Maria said. "What happened?"

"I'm not sure that I should be the one to tell you, but if he's already told you that they're dead, he must have done so for a reason. Maybe he's finally getting a little more comfortable with the fact that they're gone. I've never known Jacob to mention their death to anyone before, and I know that he'd never be capable of relating the circumstances surrounding their deaths. For Jacob, it's a very sensitive subject. I'll tell you what I know, and the next time I see him, I'll let him know that I told you."

Matt got up and moved to the stove. He picked up a cup and poured some coffee. "It happened about six years ago. Jacob had just been promoted to U.S. marshal." He moved back to the table and sat. "Because of his job, he moved nearer to Denver. Bought a little place a few miles out of town. Nice little spread. A lot like this one. It had a stream running close by the house and good grazing land. I was heading there for Little Sparrow's birthday. When I got to where I could see the house, I noticed that there was no smoke rising from the chimney, which was strange, as Songbird was always baking or cooking something. Then I saw Jacob up on a hill digging, and my heart sank. I rode up to where he was, and there were two tarpaulins lying on the ground. It was clear that he was digging two graves. I dismounted, took the shovel from him, and finished the graves. I then placed the two bodies in their final resting places. I asked him if there was anything more, and he just shook his head, so I started shoveling dirt in the graves. Suddenly, Jacob grabbed my arm and stopped me. He went to his saddlebags and rummaged around. Finally he came back carrying an eagle feather. He jumped down next to the smaller body and placed the feather carefully on the canvas. Then he moved to the second grave, removed his spirit bag from around his neck, and placed it on the tarpaulin. He stared at the body for a moment and then nodded to me. After I finished filling the graves, I moved to where Jacob was sitting. He looked at me with tears running down his cheeks and told me in a broken voice that Songbird and Little Sparrow had been raped, strangled, and scalped."

"How awful!" Maria cried.

"I don't think there's any human lower than a scalp hunter," Clay said.

"Yes, there is," said Matt. "Those that buy them."

"I'll bet Jacob went after the lowlifes that did it," Earl said.

"We stayed on the hillside that night," Matt continued. "When I woke, Jacob was already up, with his horse saddled. I asked if he wanted me to go with him. He shook his head and said that he didn't want to put his best friend outside the law, and then he rode off. I stayed on for a while, tending to the stock and cleaning up the inside of the house. After some time had passed, I was preparing to go and see if I could find him, when the head marshal from the Denver office rode in, looking for Jacob. I told him what had happened and that I was just heading out to find him. He nodded and said that when I did to tell him that his job would still be there but there would have to be a reprimand. He asked me if I knew where he might be, and I told him that Jacob would probably go to his father's—Standing Bear's— village. When I got there, I found him purifying himself in a sweat lodge." Matt stood up and poured himself another cup of coffee. "That's about all there is," he said.

Chapter Nineteen

When Matt finished, Clay, Maria, and Earl just sat there in silence, not saying a word, not knowing what to say. It was one of those times when they wished they had never asked but were glad they had. They felt closer to the man they knew as Jacob Bearson. He became, in that moment, human for them, a man who was a friend, a man who was family.

Matt got up and walked to the window. "Riders headed this way. They're too far off to make out. More than likely it's Billy and some Circle C hands, but it won't hurt to be ready if it's not."

They checked their weapons and picked their spots. Maria went in to check on Mr. Culbertson. "He's stirring a bit, but he's not conscious yet," she said when she came out. "I'm going to heat up some broth for when he wakes up."

"If those are Circle C hands, you're going to have a passel of mouths to feed," Earl said. "Better put on some beans and biscuits."

"I have a ham in the larder. I was going to fix it tonight

anyway. With potatoes and greens, there should be plenty for everyone." She went about getting things together for the evening meal. Then she put a plate of morning biscuits on the table, along with some strawberry preserves. "None of you have eaten since breakfast, so I don't guess you would object to getting rid of these old biscuits for me."

In no time the plate was empty, and they went back to watching the approaching riders. "It's the Circle C bunch all right," Earl said. "I can see Billy and his sling."

"What the hell is going on? Where am I?" Culbertson bellowed from the bedroom.

Everyone smiled. "I guess Mr. Culbertson is ready to return to the living," Clay said.

Maria fixed a bowl of broth, got a spoon from the drawer, and went into the bedroom. The others trailed after her. Culbertson was sitting up in the bed. Maria set the broth on an end table and fixed the pillows behind his back so he would be more comfortable. "You're in my father's room. You've been shot, and you shouldn't move around so much. You'll tear your wounds open." Then she handed him the broth.

The others proceeded to tell him of what they knew and all that had happened since. Clay explained how he had seen Billy shield Culbertson's body with his own. "I reckon you owe that boy a thank-you. I figure he saved your life, and he took a bullet while doing it."

"Billy did that? Where is he?"

Maria spoke up. "Mr. Stoker sent him to get a few hands from your ranch. They're riding in now and will be here soon. Now you eat that broth, and everyone else get out of here and let the man rest. I'll see that Billy comes in when he gets here." She herded them into the other room.

"Come on, Earl," Clay said. "Those Circle C men are going to want a place to put their gear and get some rest. Let's you and me see if we can turn the barn into a bunkhouse. I'll send Billy in when he gets here," he added to Maria.

She nodded and returned to the kitchen. Matt wandered around the room and then turned to the piano. "Do you mind?" he asked Maria.

She shook her head. "It would be nice to listen to someone else for a change. I don't believe I've had music while I was fixing dinner since my mother was alive, and we were still living in Ohio." Matt played while Maria busied herself in the kitchen. Drella moved to a corner, where she lay down and curled up.

Out in the barn, Clay and Earl began to make pallets to sleep on out of straw and hay. "You know, Earl," Clay said as he was busily spreading a layer of hay over a bed of straw, "I never did hear how it was that you became a deputy."

"Pretty simple, actually. My father was sheriff of Twin Forks before Gordon. He taught me to use a Colt before I learned to ride. When I was old enough, I pestered him until he took me on as his deputy."

"What happened? Did he retire?"

"Nope. He was dry-gulched. There'd been a rash of cattle rustling, and he'd gone out one afternoon to see if he could pick up the trail of them that had run off a bunch of Mr. Culbertson's beef. That evening, his horse came home still saddled and bridled. I didn't find him until the next afternoon. He'd been shot in the back. His gun was still in his holster. I don't think he ever saw who shot him and left him there to die."

"So, why didn't they make you sheriff?"

"I guess they thought I was too young. They ran notices in the papers in the region saying that the position of sheriff was available but whoever took the job had to keep the current deputy on. I guess they felt they owed my pa that much. Gordon rode into town a few days later and asked for the job. Most people knew of his cousin, judge Martin Gordon, and I guess the town council figured it wouldn't hurt to have a sheriff that had that kind of tie to the circuit judge. I don't think he was too happy to have me for a deputy, but he never made a fuss about it. We got along pretty well, although he was never very big about doing much work. He spent more time gambling than sheriffing. He won the Lucky Lady in a poker game, and the previous owner was so put out that he accused Gordon of cheating and called him out. I guess it just wasn't a very good day for him. Gordon dropped him with a single shot."

"Did they ever find out who shot your daddy?" Clay asked.

"Never did, but I still keep hoping that something will turn up that'll point to them that done it."

When the Circle C hands rode in, Clay told Billy that Culbertson wanted to see him. Billy went into the house and paused and watched with a good deal of amazement as Matt played. Finally, he said, "'Scuse me, ma'am, but they told me that Mr. Culbertson wanted to see me."

Maria turned from the stove and waved toward the bedroom. "He's in there, but if he's sleeping, it would be better if you waited until he woke."

"Yes, ma'am," Billy said, and went in to see his boss. He was in there for some time, and when he came out he just stood in the middle of the room, staring at the floor. Matt stopped playing and sat watching him for a few seconds.

"What's the matter, son?" he finally asked.

"Mr. Culbertson just made me foreman," the young man said quietly.

"That's great, Billy," Maria said.

"I think so too," Billy said. "But I'm a little scared. There's a lot of hands that've been working on the Circle C much longer than I have, and I don't know how they're going to take to me telling them what to do."

Matt got up from the piano and walked over to Billy. "You think you can do the job?" Billy nodded. Matt clapped him on the shoulder. "Then just do it. Culbertson saw something in you; the others will too. There may be some rough moments, and some will test your authority, but if you don't overreact, if you think things through before acting, and if you give everyone under your authority an honest hearing before dressing them down, you'll do just fine. The hardest part is going out there now and telling those men that came with you that Culbertson has put you in charge. Once it's been said, it'll get a whole lot easier. Just stand up straight and act like you were born to the job. The others will accept the decision because it comes from the boss. They'll accept you when they see you doing the job. You have nothing to fear. 'Cowards die many times before their deaths; the valiant only taste of death but once.' "

"I don't know what those last words you said mean," Billy said, "but they sure sounded good. Thank you, Mr. Stoker."

"You're welcome, Billy. Now go on out and show everyone what you're made of."

Maria and Matt watched through the window as Billy went out to talk to the Circle C hands. "He's going to do just fine," Matt said. "Look how he's standing, erect and positive. He's also talking to them quietly and in a non-confrontational manner. I do believe Mr. Culbertson has made a very good choice."

"He certainly is giving the appearance of confidence," Maria said. "For a minute here in the house, I wasn't so sure. Well, I can't stand here gawking out the window." She turned back toward the kitchen. "Those men are going to be expecting to eat any time now."

"Anything I can do to help?"

"Yes, you can play some more. Music makes the work easier and more enjoyable."

Matt returned to the piano. Meanwhile, Billy was telling the men what was expected of them, and he, along with Clay and Earl, showed them where they could store their blankets and other gear. He told the men that he wanted to keep guards on throughout the night, just to be on the safe side. Now that he was in charge, he didn't want anything to happen to Mr. Culbertson. He felt that to fail in his first act of responsibility was the worst thing that could occur. He was still a little frightened of the position he had been placed in, even though he didn't think it showed, but he knew he had a lot of growing to do before he would be comfortable in the role of foreman of the Circle C. He wished he had the self-assurance of a man like Matthew Stoker.

In the house, Matt played while Maria went about preparing the evening meal. She knew they would eat later than normal, but given all that had happened, there was no way around it. Drella remained in the corner, but every now and then she would raise her head and look around and listen. After the better part of an hour, Maria went to the door and called out to Earl to tell the men that supper was ready. Then she returned to the kitchen and fixed a tray for Mr. Culbertson and took it in to the bedroom. Earl, Clay, Billy, and three of the Circle C hands came in and sat themselves around the table. Matt joined them as Maria came out of the bedroom. She placed platters of food on the table and told them that Culbertson had wanted to come out and join them, but she had convinced him that he should stay in bed for now.

The meal was attacked by the men with hearty appetites, but in silence. Finally, Billy spoke up. "Pete, I want you and Jimmy to go out and relieve Tad and Sid when you're through. In about three hours, Stan and me will take over for you."

The men nodded, mopped up the juices on their plates with a biscuit, tossed off their coffee, and pushed their chairs back. "Thank you, ma'am," Pete said. "That was a mighty fine meal."

"You're welcome," Maria replied. "It's the least I could do for all your help."

The three hands grabbed their hats and headed out the door. Billy got up and started toward the bedroom, saying, "It's the least *we* can do, ma'am, seeing as how the Circle C is responsible for some if not all of your problems. Mr. Culbertson told me earlier that we was to do whatever we could for you. And here you go and fix one of the best meals any of us has ever had." Billy went into the bedroom before Maria could reply.

Matt pushed his chair back and got up. "They're right, Maria. It has been a long time since I've had such an elegant supper."

Maria blushed and turned back to the stove. She prepared a plate of ham and potatoes and put it on the floor. "I bet you thought I forgot all about you, Drella. Okay, girl." Drella got up and moved to the plate.

Matt followed the Circle C hands out, sat down on the porch steps, and rolled himself a smoke. Drella had finished eating and followed him out. In a few moments, the other two Circle C hands came up to the porch. Matt told them to go inside and that supper was waiting. Drella watched the two men enter the house, and then she lay down beside Matt, taking great interest in a sow bug as it made its way across the bottom step. Matt leaned back against a post and took in the night sky, giving the appearance of a man at ease, but his mind was still grappling with the events of the last several days and why they had occurred. Drella's tail thumped the porch as Clay came out and joined Matt on the stairs. The three of them sat in silence for a time. Then Drella got up, walked down the stairs, and stuck her head under the porch where she had seen the sow bug disappear. The two men watched her in amusement. Finally, Clay broke the silence.

"Matthew, what in the hell is going on around here? There is way too much happening for no recognizable reason."

"Damned if I know for sure, but I think it's some sort of land grab. Jacob told me that the railroad's going to be putting a spur through this part of the country. But I can't say for sure who's behind all that's happening."

"Well, I can tell you that I'm out of here when this is over," Clay said. "I do believe I have worn out my welcome in Twin Forks—if I ever had one."

"What do you plan on doing?"

"I'll probably just drift until I can hook on somewhere. No matter what they tell you, the war didn't make life a whole lot better for people like me. What about you? Where are you headed after all this is over?"

"I was headed for Colorado when I rode into this valley. I purchased a ranch near a town called Ovid. I've transferred most of my money to a bank there owned by a man named Wendell Randolph. He's arranged for a couple to look after the place until I get there. I don't know if folks will let me do it, but I'm going to try to put my present life behind me."

"You'll make it, Matthew. A man can do most anything once he puts his mind to it."

They sat in silence for a while longer, and then Matt said, "Why don't you come in with me, Clay? Between the two of us, we could have a good life."

"I can't go partners with you. I don't have more than two dollars to my name. And I don't respond well to charity."

"I'm not offering charity, Clay. You work the ranch a couple of years for no wages and you will have earned your partnership. It would be a whole lot better than drifting and selling yourself to those that would hire you, probably for less money than they're paying their other hands."

"That's true enough. I'll think about it, Matthew. And I thank you for the offer."

Chapter Twenty

A re you certain you got him?" Sheriff Gordon asked. He was sitting behind his desk with his feet up.

"He went down like a steer in a slaughterhouse," Curly said. He was bandaging Sam's arm. "It's just a flesh wound, but the way you hollered, I thought you was mortally wounded." He turned to Gordon and said, "Culbertson must have been hit by two or three shots, and we was all aiming to kill. We don't have to worry about him anymore, but there was more in the house than we figured on, so you best put together a large posse and tell them to take no chances and shoot to kill."

The sheriff kicked his feet from the desk and stood up. "Don't you worry none about the posse. They'll do what I tell 'em, but they take orders better when they're full of courage, so you and Buster better get down to the Lucky Lady and keep it pouring. Don't say nothing about Culbertson. I'll come down in a bit and announce that the gunfighter and those out at the Johnson place have gunned him down in cold blood. You just tell folks that it's your birthday or something and buy several drinks for everyone there. Here's some cash. Sam, you best sit this one out. Go back and use one of the cells and get some rest."

"We'll keep anyone there going, but you'd better see that they're really lathered up when they leave, or they're going to start thinking about going up against a man who makes his living using a gun," Curly said as he and Buster headed toward the door.

"Don't you worry," the sheriff said. "I know how to handle the sheep in this town."

Jacob found the place where the ambushers had hidden themselves and followed their trail to where they'd staked out their horses. He found a few drops of blood where one of the mounts had been tied. "Looks like the kid did hit one of them," he muttered to himself. He swung into the saddle and began to follow the trail that had been left by the bushwhackers.

"You know, Mischief, these fellows don't seem very concerned about whether or not they'd be followed. Why do you think that is?" The buckskin pricked her ears at the sound of his voice and reached down to grab a tuft of grass. She had learned long ago that when her rider started talking, she could get away with grabbing a mouthful or two as they went along. "Either they're not very bright, which is a real possibility, or they don't think they have any reason to worry, or maybe both."

Jacob pulled her head up and urged her on at a swift

single-foot walk. When they reached the road to Twin Forks, Jacob pulled up. "They probably rode straight into town," Jacob said, "but I think I'll check the other side just to be certain. If they went into town, they'll still be there when we get in."

Jacob checked the other side of the road for a couple hundred yards in each direction. Finding no sign, he guided Mischief into the road and let her head toward town at her own pace. "Probably won't find any way to identify them, but I might get some idea of what's going on if I nose around a bit. What do you think, old girl?" Mischief just moved along at a steady pace, somewhat disappointed that she was on a well-traveled road with nothing to forage. "In any case, it'll give me a chance to give you a breather and maybe a nosebag of grain."

As Jacob rode through the town, he noticed nothing out of the ordinary. He rode to the livery stable and found an empty stall. He left the roan saddled but loosened the girth. He found a nosebag and put in a couple of scoops of oats. On his way out, he dropped a dollar in a pad-locked box by the front door, per instructions on the sign above it. Then he started across the street toward the Lucky Lady, which seemed to be doing a thriving business. He pushed through the batwings and moved to the corner of the bar nearest the entrance and away from the center of activity. No one took any notice of him as he came in. He ordered a beer, and when he went to pay for it, the bartender shook his head.

"No charge," he said.

"How come?"

"It's Curly Williams' birthday, and all the drinks are on him."

Jacob smiled and nodded. As he sipped his beer, he let his eyes roam around the room. Everyone seemed to be having a good time, and nothing seemed out of the ordinary. Still, Jacob was struck by the fact that such revelry was occurring on the heels of an attempted murder, and the marshal was not a great believer in coincidence.

Just then the sheriff stepped into the bar. He didn't notice Jacob in the corner. He lifted his voice above the din. "Hold it down!" he shouted. "I've got some bad news." Slowly, a hush fell over the room. "I've just been told that John Culbertson has been murdered, gunned down by that gunfighter Stoker out at the Johnson place. I want as many of you as possible to go home and get your guns and ride with me as a posse out to the Johnson ranch and bring that killer in, dead or alive. Have a couple of drinks on me and then get moving. We'll be riding in forty-five minutes."

As the crush of men moved toward the bar, Jacob quietly moved toward the front door. When he reached it and stepped through, he turned back and watched the sheriff move to a table where two other ranch hands were sitting. He was pretty sure he had seen them out at the Culbertson spread when he had visited on earlier occasions. Jacob walked across to the stable and tightened up the cinch on Mischief. "Sorry to interrupt your meal, old friend, but we've got to get out and warn Matthew." He swung up into the saddle, rode out of the stable, and turned Mischief toward the Johnson ranch.

Back in the Lucky Lady, Curly, Buster, and the sheriff were quietly congratulating themselves on the way they had handled things.

Chapter Twenty-one

Matt and Clay were still on the porch, enjoying the evening and getting to know each other. They both got up as one of the lookouts was coming toward the house. It was Pete.

"Rider coming in," he said. "Looks like he's coming from town. Is Billy inside?" Clay nodded, and Pete went in.

Matt moved to the side of the house and loosened his Colt in the holster. Drella followed him. "Only one, so I don't think it's anything serious, but it can't hurt to be careful."

Clay reached inside the front door and grabbed his rifle. He moved into the shadows on the other side of the house. Billy opened the door and stood in the doorway.

"You make a hell of a target framed in that light," Matt said. Billy jumped to the side of the door. Matt noted with satisfaction that he didn't go back inside. He stared hard in the direction the rider would be coming from. Finally, the rider appeared outlined against the night sky, Drella's tail started wagging, and Matt smiled and walked out of the shadows. "It's all right. It's just Jacob. He's coming at a faster pace than normal, so it must be important."

Billy opened the door and said, "It's the marshal." Maria and the others came out onto the porch as Jacob was riding in, and Clay stepped out of the shadows where he had positioned himself. Jacob laughed when he saw Clay.

"I must be getting old," he said as he dismounted. "I figured your location, Matthew, and I saw young Billy step from the door into the shadows on the porch, but I didn't pick out Clay at all. Had I been a bad guy, you'd have had me for sure."

"Come on inside and get something to eat, Marshal," Maria said. "You must be starved."

"That I am, ma'am. My belly button's pressing against my backbone. Matthew, I have some news, and you're not going to like it."

Everyone followed the marshal into the house except Pete, who went back to his lookout position. Maria placed a big plate of food on the table in front of Jacob and poured him a cup of coffee. Jacob dug into the food with gusto. After a couple of mouthfuls, he took a large swallow of coffee and turned to Matt. "I followed the tracks all the way to town. There wasn't much hope of locating the bushwhackers, but I thought I'd hit the Lucky Lady and see if I could hear anything that might help. The place was jumping because it was somebody's birthday, and he was buying drinks for everyone. Then the sheriff came in. He said that John Culbertson had been gunned down by you, Matthew, and that he wanted a posse to help him come out here and get you." Jacob looked at Maria and said, "This food is the best I've had since my wife passed on."

Maria blushed. "I'm very flattered, Marshal."

"Anyway, I figured that I had better hightail it back here and let you know what's going on. There's a posse coming, and they're getting good and liquored up."

"But, Marshal," Maria said, "Mr. Stoker came in with you!"

"Yes, ma'am, but the bushwhackers didn't know that. I guess they figured Matthew was here and that Culbertson was dead. How's he doing, anyhow?"

A voice from the bedroom hollered, "I'm doing fine! Will someone please tell me what in hell's going on?"

Maria went into the bedroom and, after a few moments, came out. "He wants to see you and Mr. Stoker, Marshal. Billy, he wants you to come along too."

"I thought we got past this 'Marshal' business some time ago."

"I'm sorry. He wants to see you, Jacob."

"That's better. 'Marshal' makes me sound too damned officious, pardon my language, Maria."

The three of them went into the bedroom. Culbertson was sitting up in bed, propped up by some pillows. Jacob walked up to him and stuck out his hand. "John, you look pretty good for someone who's dead."

Culbertson laughed as he shook the marshal's hand. "I guess I'm just too ornery to lie down. But seriously, you think they'll be coming out after Stoker?"

Jacob nodded. "I'm sure of it, but I can handle it. Still, I'd like to know who told them you were shot by Matthew. Most certainly that person was among the ambushers."

"I have some suspicions of my own as to who was behind that," Culbertson said. "I paid my foreman off earlier today. He'd been doing some things without my knowing, and I would be surprised if he wasn't involved in some fashion." Culbertson then turned his attention to Matt. "Mr. Stoker, I understand that you're responsible for patching me up. I'm mighty grateful but somewhat surprised given your attitude when we met earlier today."

"As I told you then, Mr. Culbertson, I wasn't certain that you were behind what's been going on. If you were, I wanted to put you on notice that I'd taken a hand."

"That's what I figured," Culbertson said. "I've already apologized to Miss Johnson and explained to her that I had no idea what Curly and the others had been up to. I also told her that, as the owner of the Circle C, I was responsible for whatever my hands did and that I hoped she would let me make it up to her. And I figure that I owe you for the doctoring."

"What I did for you, I would have done for anyone. Despite what some have said of me, I do not relish any man dying. But if you don't mind my saying so, I think there's more to your being shot than simply the anger of a foreman who was fired. I think someone has a reason to want you dead."

"Maybe so," Culbertson said. "I've been thinking about that since I woke up. Lord knows I've made some enemies. But I don't believe any of them would've let someone else have the pleasure of killing me."

"Matthew and I have been thinking about all that's been happening," Jacob broke in, "and we've come up with some ideas. Who would get your ranch if you died? Have you made out a will?"

"No, I haven't, but I will before I leave this bed," Culbertson said. "I suppose the county would get the Circle C. I have no living relatives that I know of."

"Jacob tells me that the railroad's planning to put a spur through this part of the country," Matt said, "and he and I believe someone's trying to corner the land so they can make a tidy profit from the railroad company. Our problem is that we can go no further. The whole deal was supposed to be kept secret to prevent the very thing that seems to be happening."

"Well, it certainly was kept a secret from me!" Culbertson said, obviously surprised. "I had no idea they were planning a spur, although I have to admit that it would make shipping my beef a whole lot easier."

"It's a puzzle," Jacob said. "But we have more immediate problems. That posse from town will be here any minute. I plan to tell them that Matthew's in my custody and then see if I can get the sheriff in here to see that you aren't dead. I suspect he'll still want to take you in for the Johnson killing, Matthew, but I'll handle that somehow."

"Just tell him that I'll come in to his office tomorrow. I tell you, Jacob, that I don't mind you saying that I'm in your custody, but under the circumstances, I'm not giving you my gun."

"Have I asked you for it? But if you shoot anyone without provocation, you'll have to shoot me too."

Both men knew that each had his pride and each had his own way of doing things. The words didn't have to be spoken, but sometimes they spoke them anyway as a reminder of who each of them were. Billy had just been standing against the bedroom wall, taking everything in. He wasn't sure he understood everything they were talking about, but he was proud to be included in the group of men in the room.

"Did you want to speak to me, Mr. Culbertson?" he asked finally, struggling to keep his voice from trembling.

"Yes, son, I did," Culbertson replied. "I want you to make certain that the Circle C riders know whose hand they are backing. Not only those that are already here, but others who might have been in town when the posse was being formed. Not Curly and the other two, of course, but any others that might be along for the ride will need to understand that they either stand with the marshal or they no longer work for the Circle C. You think you can handle that?"

"Yes, sir. I'll see to it."

"Good, Billy," Culbertson said. "I want this ranch and the people here protected at all costs. I've already been responsible for more problems here than I care to think about. I can't bring Henry back from the grave, but I can try to make sure that no further damage is done to his daughter or his—um, her—place."

There was a knock on the door, and Earl stuck his head in. "Riders coming in. They're about five minutes out."

Matt, Jacob, and Billy started out, when Culbertson

said, "Will you ask Miss Johnson if I can have some paper and a pen?"

Jacob stopped, turned, and said, "I'll see to it. You just take it easy, John."

"Thanks, and you be careful out there."

Jacob walked into the other room and saw that only Earl and Maria were there. "Where is everyone?"

Maria and Earl both pointed toward the door. Jacob opened it. The moon was nearly three quarters full, and Jacob could see fairly well. He saw Billy by the corral, talking to the Circle C hands, but he couldn't see hide nor hair of Clay, Matt, or Drella. He looked up and saw that the posse was about a hundred yards out. He turned his head and said, "Earl, come on out here. Maria, I think it's best that you stay inside. Oh, yeah, Culbertson would like some paper and something to write with."

Earl joined Jacob on the porch. Jacob said to him, "As of now you are a temporary deputy U.S. marshal. Just stand here beside me. Don't do anything unless you see me go for my gun. If that happens, you're on your own, so if I was you I would start looking for places that could provide cover. I don't think we'll have any problems, but I've been wrong before."

Earl began sizing up the area. "Looks like the best place for cover is behind you." He smiled.

"You're probably right, but I don't think it'll last very long. Better be looking to dive somewhere else."

Chapter Twenty-two

The posse rode into the yard, with Sheriff Gordon at its head. Jacob made a quick count and came up with fifteen. They spaced themselves across the front of the house. Billy and the Circle C hands were slightly behind them to the left by the corral. Curly and a couple of others turned their mounts so as to keep the men by the corral in sight. The sheriff rode out a yard or two in front of the others.

"Evening, Marshal. We're here for the man who murdered John Culbertson and probably Henry Johnson."

"And who might that be?" Jacob asked.

"The gunslinger Stoker."

"Maybe you better step down and we'll talk about it."

"The time for talking's over. Get him out here."

Jacob saw that Billy was standing between a couple of members of the group, talking to them quietly. He watched as Billy turned and went back to the corral and the riders slowly backed their mounts out of line, rode over to the corral, and dismounted. *Odds are changing,* he thought to himself. Turning his attention back to Gordon, he said, "Matthew Stoker is in my custody, Sheriff. Come inside, and we'll have a little chat about whether or not you can talk to him."

"Damn it, Marshal! This is my jurisdiction. You get Stoker out here or we'll get him ourselves." There were murmurs of agreement from the other members of the group.

"You have to do what you think is best," Jacob said to the group. "But I said he was in my custody. I didn't say I'd taken his gun from him, and I didn't say he was inside. I also didn't say he was alone. If I was a member of your posse, I'd take a look around at what I see and, more important, what I don't see, and then I'd try to encourage my leader to go inside and have a talk with the U.S. marshal whose jurisdiction supersedes the sheriff's."

The men on horseback began to look around. They noted the men by the corral, and they saw that Earl had moved down to the edge of the porch. They twisted their heads one way and another but couldn't see Matt anywhere. Jacob could see that they were getting nervous. Finally, the storekeeper, Higgens, spoke up. "Maybe you better do like he says, Sheriff. It can't hurt to talk. We're not backing down, but we should explore every avenue before we turn to force."

Gordon himself had noted that there was more apparent opposition than he'd first realized. He swung his considerable bulk from the saddle. "All right, Marshal, we'll have your little chat."

"Good," Jacob said. "The rest of you just stay where

you are and try to relax a little. Earl here, whom I have deputized, by the way, will see to it that no harm comes to you."

Jacob turned, opened the door, and went inside. The sheriff followed, and Jacob closed the door. Jacob motioned to the table, and both men sat down. Maria set a cup in front of each of them and poured them some coffee.

"Good evening, Sheriff. Do you want any cream or sugar?"

The sheriff pushed the cup into the center of the table, sloshing some of the coffee over the rim. "I didn't come in here for any tea party. Where's Stoker?"

"There's no need to be rude, Gordon," Jacob said. "We'll get to Matthew Stoker's whereabouts in a few minutes. But first, where did you get the information about Culbertson's demise?"

"I don't know. Some drover said he was passing and saw the whole thing."

"Does this drover have a name?"

"I don't know his name. Look, Marshal, there has been a murder, and I want the man responsible."

"I'm sure you do, but Matthew Stoker's not that man. He was with me when we heard the shots, and we both rode in together. Your witness must have good eyes to see the shooters when they were hidden in the trees. I really would like to talk with this person."

"Well, if it wasn't the gunfighter that killed Culbertson, who was it?"

"I don't know who did the shooting, but I tracked three riders from here to town. I suspect that the person who told you he saw it is one of them, but, of course, you don't remember who that was. If I were a suspicious man, I might think you had a hand in gunning down Culbertson."

"Me!" Gordon shouted. "I'm the law. U.S. marshal or not, you'd better watch yourself, Bearson. Now, who do you think murdered Culbertson?"

"You're just not having a good day, Sheriff. Culbertson's not dead. He's in the bedroom there, recuperating from his wounds. I'll take you in to see him in a minute, but first, you're going to stop this nonsense about blaming Stoker for everything from spitting on the boardwalk to murder. If you want to talk to him about what he knows, he'll be glad to meet with you. But if you're simply going to use him as a scapegoat, I'll see to it that you never get a chance to talk with him."

Sheriff Gordon sat in silence. He reached across the table and picked up his coffee cup and took a sip. Jacob noted that Gordon's hand was shaking. Finally, the sheriff said, "Maybe I was leaping to conclusions. Stoker's reputation makes him an easy target. I would like to talk to him, though."

"Fine, I'll see to it that he comes in tomorrow. Now, let's go in and see Culbertson, and then you can take that mob outside back to town."

They went into the bedroom, and the sheriff talked with Culbertson for a few minutes. Culbertson told him what he remembered about the attack, and he told him that he did not know who the bushwhackers were. Then the two lawmen returned to the posse outside, and Sheriff Gordon explained to them that Culbertson was not dead and that Matt was not a suspect in the ambush but would be coming into town to talk with the sheriff about what he knew of the attack on Culbertson and the death of Henry Johnson. The sheriff mounted his horse, and the posse followed him out of the yard and back toward town.

Matt and Drella stepped out of the shadows. Jacob noted that the hair on the back of the dog was standing up.

Matt moved over to stand next to Jacob. "Did you see Drella?" Jacob asked.

"Yes, I did. There was someone in that group that she wasn't very happy with."

"Yeah, and in the past her judgment has been better than yours or mine."

"Very true, my friend, very true. Let's get inside and see what we've learned, if anything. Billy, Clay, Earl, come on inside." Matt looked down at Drella. "Yes, you can come in too, and I wish you could talk. I suspect you knew that the bushwhackers were in that posse."

Chapter Twenty-three

Maria had already set out the coffee cups and filled them, and by each cup was a generous slice of pie. "I baked some pies a couple of days ago, but with all that's been going on, I forgot about them." She turned to take a piece into the bedroom, when the door opened and John Culbertson hobbled out. "You get back in that bed," she scolded.

"I've had enough pampering. I'll be all right. Besides, I have something I want to talk to you about."

They made a place for him at the table, and he reached into his shirt pocket and pulled out some folded paper. "As I promised, I made out my will. I need a couple of witnesses, and as it concerns some of you here, I want to discuss it with all of you."

Culbertson took a bite of pie and washed it down with coffee. "Damn, this is good, Maria. If young Earl here wasn't so handy with a Colt, I believe I'd start courting you myself." Earl's neck turned red, and he suddenly became very interested in the pie on his plate. Culbertson chuckled. "I believe I've embarrassed the lad. Now then, about my will, I want all of you to realize that this will is subject to change, but for now, I've made William here my heir." Billy's mouth dropped open in surprise. "I know this is out of the blue, son, but at the moment you're the only person at the ranch I can be certain isn't going to try to put me six feet under. I also believe that if I were to marry and have a child, you'd be happy for me and wouldn't be bothered if the will were changed. I think you know that I would take care of you. After all, I owe you my life." Now it was Billy's turn to stare at his plate as color rose in his face.

"From what I've seen today, Mr. Culbertson," Maria said as she rose from the table, "you've made a very good choice. I think I'll take a couple slices of pie to the men outside."

"Can it wait a minute, Miss Johnson?" Culbertson asked. "I have more to say, and it concerns you." Maria returned to her chair. "In the event that William here jumps in front of more bullets intended for me or anyone else, I've left the Circle C to you." It was Maria's turn to be surprised. She started to protest, but Culbertson raised his hand. "Hear me out. Although unwittingly, I've been responsible for causing you and Henry a lot of grief, and maybe my failure to pay attention to what was going on might have been partially responsible for your father's death. You're a good woman, Maria, and I know that should anything happen to Billy or me, you would see to it that the Circle C would continue on in a way that I would approve of."

"I don't know what to say," Maria said.

Clay broke the brief silence that followed. "I commend you, Mr. Culbertson. I don't think there are two better people around here to protect what you've built. I'm sure that neither Billy nor Miss Johnson would let anything bad happen to the Circle C. Your legacy will be secure. I don't know of anyone else around here I could say that about."

"Thank you, Clay. Those are my feelings exactly. Now if you, Jacob, Earl, and Mr. Stoker will sign as witnesses."

The document was passed around the table, and each man signed in turn. Then Culbertson folded it and put it in his pocket, telling the others that he would file it the next time he was in town. That prompted Matt to ask where he would file it, as he hadn't seen a courthouse. Culbertson explained that Higgens at the general store had a strong box in which important documents could be placed until the circuit judge came by. He added that the circuit judge was Sheriff Gordon's cousin and came to town every couple of months.

"That's very interesting," Matt said, and he looked at Jacob. "That would be an individual who could have access to political inside information."

"Worth looking into," Jacob said.

"You mean about the railroad spur?" Culbertson asked, and both men nodded. "Well, that may be, but I've known Judge Gordon for a long time, and I'd stake my life on him being an honest and honorable man."

"I know him too, and I agree with you," Jacob said. "However, the judge does like his bourbon and might well have let a confidence slip if he were enjoying the benefits of the Lucky Lady and the generosity of his cousin."

Culbertson thought for a moment. "That's true. He does enjoy his bourbon, and I can't say the sheriff shares the judge's character traits. In fact, in that area I would say they were total opposites."

"You think he has some money salted away?" Jacob asked.

"The sheriff? I wouldn't be surprised. The saloon turns a tidy profit, and he keeps all fines that are legally imposed. One of the perks of being the sheriff."

"Would he also know that you have no relatives?" Matt asked.

"I believe I've mentioned it to him on more than one occasion," Culbertson replied.

"If that's so, it would be no problem to get from the judge whether or not you had filed a will," Jacob said. "Matthew, I'm thinking that maybe you shouldn't go in to see Gordon tomorrow. It might be a trap."

"Could be, but even if it is, I think we should go ahead. He might make a play and show his hand. If we expect a trap, it shouldn't be too hard to avoid getting caught in it if we plan our moves carefully."

"All of this is very interesting," Maria said, "but Mr. Culbertson is looking very tired and should get back to bed. If anything's going to happen tomorrow, he's not going to be a part of it."

Culbertson protested, but Jacob assured him that he'd tell Culbertson what they were planning before they went to town. Maria ushered the reluctant Circle C owner back to the bedroom. The others sat at the table for another hour, working out the details of what they would do the next day. Then they said good night to Maria and headed out to the barn. Although they expected no more trouble, it had been decided that Billy would keep the Circle C hands on guard for the rest of the night, just to be safe.

Chapter Twenty-four

Y ou no longer have a problem with Culbertson.' That's what you said." Sheriff Gordon was pacing around his office. Curly, Sam, and Buster were standing there, looking very uncomfortable. "Why in the hell didn't you wait around to find out for certain that he was dead? Now I got that son-of-a-bitching marshal pestering me for the name of the person who told me he was dead. Can't you guys do anything right?" he snarled as he sank into his chair.

"You was happy enough with us when we run those other squatters off," Curly said. "And you didn't seem too upset when we helped you dry-gulch Sheriff Burns. Actually, we've been damn lucky something hasn't gone wrong before. All we have to do now is figure out how to fix it."

"You made me look like such an idiot," Gordon retorted. "Things were going fine because no one tied me in with what was happening. Now I'm not so sure. That marshal is nobody's fool."

"We can handle the marshal," Sam spoke up. "We can

151

waylay him out in the open when he isn't expecting anything."

"Oh, that's really smart. You can't kill a man when he's sitting still right in front of you, and you're going to try and take an experienced lawman straight on?" Gordon got up from his chair and walked over to them. He poked Sam in the chest with his finger. "I'll tell you what you're going to do. You're going to do exactly what I tell you to do." He turned to the window and gazed out for several minutes. The others looked at him and then at each other. Curly shrugged his shoulders at Sam and Buster. Finally, the sheriff turned back to them.

"We need to take each problem one at a time. Culbertson can wait. We'll always have an opportunity to get him. The gunfighter and the marshal are our immediate problem. The marshal told me that he'd see to it that Stoker would come in tomorrow. We'll take them here in town. You stake out hiding places on both sides of the office across the street. Let them come into the office. I'll ask a couple of questions about Johnson's death and then tell them I'm sorry for the trouble and that they can go. When they come out of the office, we'll be on all four sides. Nobody's that good. They won't know where to shoot first, and by the time they decide, they'll be dead."

"What if Stoker comes in alone?" Curly asked.

"All the better. We'll only have one target, and there'll still be four of us. Then we'll deal with the marshal and Culbertson later. The gunfighter's the wild card. He doesn't have to play by anyone's rules. Get him first and the rest will be easier."

The three men looked at the sheriff and then nodded in agreement to the plan. "Let's go down to the Lucky Lady and have a drink to a successful day tomorrow," Curly said. The four of them headed out the door. On the way to the saloon, they all considered possible hiding places for the ambush.

Chapter Twenty-five

Breakfast at the Johnson place was good but very subdued compared to a normal ranch morning meal. Billy had told the Circle C hands about the suspicions they had and what was being done about them. He had told them that they would be staying at the Johnson place and that lookouts would continue to be posted until Mr. Culbertson was ready to travel. Culbertson himself joined the group at the table for breakfast and told Billy that he wanted him to make certain that the roundup and branding were continuing. He also told him to have the cook begin to lay in supplies for the coming drive to market. Billy said he would go and see to it that the work was assigned and that the hands were doing their jobs. He would come back later and release a couple of other hands to return to the ranch.

After eating, Matt, Clay, and Jacob took their coffee out on the porch, rolled smokes, and discussed the trip into town. Earl had indicated that he wanted to come along, but Matt had told him that he had better stay with Maria, at least until Billy returned from the Circle C.

"You know," Jacob said, "that Earl is a pretty good kid. I may ask that he be given permanent status as a deputy. Then he could use this area as his headquarters and kill two birds with one stone."

"Why, Jacob," Clay laughed, "where's your bow and arrow? Although I always figured Cupid to be better looking."

Matt let out a laugh, and Jacob took his hat off and swung it at Clay's head. Maria came out at that moment with the coffeepot. "I don't understand you," she said. "Here you are playing games when you're about to walk into what you know is a trap."

" 'Eat, drink, and make merry,' " Matt said. "What has to be done has to be done, Maria. There's nothing to be gained by worrying about it. Worry too much and you lose your edge."

"But you could get killed."

"That's right, Maria, and so could others. Jacob, Clay, and I aren't happy about what may lie ahead, nor do we take it lightly, but that's all the more reason to seize the moment. Men who have a gun as the tool of their trade cannot afford to let time pass unnoticed or fail to enjoy the moments of peace that they have. Their work is too demanding and uncertain."

"Well, I think it's terrible work."

"Would you rather that the men who killed your father and attacked John Culbertson be allowed to get away with it?"

"No, but I wish there were another way." Maria turned and went back inside.

"So do I," Matt said. "So do I."

Jacob and Clay walked over beside Matt. "Maybe I won't see about making that deputy job permanent," Jacob said.

"I think you should go ahead, Jacob," Matt said. "The time has not yet come that you can afford not to hire the best you can. Let it be his and Maria's decision."

Billy came out on the porch, followed by Earl. "I'm headed over to the Circle C. The men here have their lookout assignments. Those not on lookout will be keeping an eye out or getting some rest in the barn. They all know that they're to protect Mr. Culbertson and Miss Johnson no matter what."

"That's good," Jacob said. "Matthew, Clay, and I will be heading for town shortly, and we'll certainly feel better knowing there's someone keeping an eye on this place."

"Miss Johnson said she'll take care of meals, but she's running short on some supplies. Mr. Culbertson told me to get some from the ranch, so I might be gone a little longer than I thought I would."

"That's okay," Matt said. "Earl here will keep watch over those inside. Even though I trust your judgment, Billy, I want Earl to stay inside. Some of these hands may still feel some loyalty to Curly. Especially those who came in with the posse last night."

"I still think I should go to town with you and the marshal," Earl said. "Clay could stay and guard the house.

I know the layout of the town. If things aren't normal, I'll know it."

"Sorry, Earl," Matt said. "The main point is that you are the law. Jacob will be with us. I want a lawman here as well. If a question of legality arises, your presence will be important."

Billy agreed. "I sure will feel better if any shooting starts knowing that a deputy is here."

"I'm pretty certain that the sheriff has removed me as a deputy by now."

"But I haven't," Jacob said. "In fact, when I get back to the office, I'm thinking about getting your appointment made permanent. That is, if you want it."

"Want it?" Earl said. "You bet I want it!"

"What about Maria?" Jacob asked. "She may not go for the idea of you taking on a job that makes you a target."

Earl hung his head for a moment. "That's true," he said, "but I'm already a deputy—or was—and I've never wanted anything more than to be a lawman. She'll just have to understand. I'll make her understand. I've got to make her understand."

"Well, I'd better get going," Billy said and started toward the barn. Then he stopped and came back. "Mr. Stoker, I sure do want to apologize for the way I acted at the Lucky Lady, and I also want to thank you for the way you dealt with me. Not many would've let such a fool off the hook."

"Forget it, son. It's over. But I hope you learned that liquor isn't much help in a situation like that."

"Don't you worry none. I learned that lesson for sure."

They watched as Billy walked toward the barn. "There goes a man that wears responsibility well," Earl said. "Just a few days ago I thought he was one of the biggest hell-raisers at the Circle C."

"Circumstance will always show a man's true colors," Matt said. "I don't think Billy changed much. I just think this is the first time he's had the opportunity to let the real man inside come to the surface." He turned to Jacob and Clay. "We'd better get ready to go. We don't want Sheriff Gordon to think we forgot about our appointment."

The three men chuckled and headed to the barn to get their gear. They caught and saddled their mounts and led them to the house. They tied them to the porch rail and went inside. Culbertson was sitting in an easy chair, and Maria, as usual, was busy in the kitchen. Earl was sitting at the table, looking like a lost puppy. The three men looked at Culbertson, and he laughed. "Lovers' quarrel," he said.

"Lovers, humph!" Maria said as she banged a kettle in the sink.

"We're on our way," Matt said. "Jacob has deputized Earl, so if anything happens while we're gone, you let him handle it, and do as he says. I don't think we'll be gone very long, but if we are, don't start worrying. It may only mean that things have taken a little longer to get settled."

"You three be careful," Culbertson said. "I truly hope we're wrong and you're not walking into a trap. But if you are, watch your back. None of those boys, including Gordon, are above back shooting."

"Do you have to go?" Maria asked. "Isn't there some

other way? I don't want any of you shot. Not on my account."

"It has gone way beyond just you, Maria," Matt said. "Your father and John here are just the most obvious victims. If our suspicions are correct, there have been other homesteaders involved, and other actions might well stir up the Indian tribes. Clay, Jacob, and I know what we're doing. The time's coming when there will be no place for men like us and young Earl here, but that time isn't here yet. Until it gets here, folks like you and John need some help. That's what we do—help folks who need it. You have a right to live the life you want without fear. Sometimes it takes men like us to see to it that your right to live as you please is protected. You can never tell about people just by looks or titles. A U.S. marshal, a former slave, and a gunfighter are an unlikely trio for respectable people to be turning to, but the need is here, and so are we. Deep inside you wouldn't have us turn our backs, would you?"

"I guess not, but I wish there was another way."

" 'If wishes were horses, beggars would ride.' Time to go, Drella." With that, Matt tipped his hat to Maria and walked out. Drella, who had been sleeping in the corner, got up, stretched with her front feet forward and then her back legs out, yawned, and followed Matt out the door. The two other men followed, all three mounted, and they rode off toward town, with the dog trotting just in front of Aphrodite. Maria, tears running down her cheeks, watched through the window until they were out of sight. Then she turned toward Earl, walked over, and sat beside him.

"I'm sorry, Earl. I never thought I'd want you to be a marshal, but if it's what you want, then I want it too. But you have to promise me that when that time comes that Matthew talked about, you'll quit and put your gun away for good."

"I do promise, Maria, and I truly hope that time comes sooner than later."

"Now, you young people stop your fretting. Those three have been around for quite a while, and I imagine they'll be around for a good deal longer," Culbertson said. "Maria, may I have some more of that excellent coffee you brew?"

Chapter Twenty-six

Curly, Sam, and Buster were having breakfast with the sheriff at the Lucky Lady. The three had chosen their positions, and Sheriff Gordon had checked out each one and was satisfied. They were talking in low voices, making their final plans.

"I don't know when they'll be coming in, so you boys may be hiding for some time. On your way out, go to the kitchen and get some food to tide you over in case they don't come into town until late. But no whiskey till it's over. The last thing we need is for any of you to be seeing double. Get the job done, and drinks will be on the house."

"You worry too much, Gordon," Curly said. "We know what's expected of us. You just make damn sure that you remember how much we've done for you. You forget your promises, and we may just turn to bushwhacking one more time."

"You don't scare me, Curly, and anyway, I don't have

any plans to cut you out. Now you better get going. They might be early risers."

The three got up and walked toward the kitchen. The sheriff watched them until they were out of sight and then nodded toward the barkeep and pointed to his coffee cup. The barkeep hollered to the swamper, who came out of the kitchen with a pot of coffee, poured some in the sheriff's cup, and went back to the kitchen. Gordon pulled a cheroot from his vest pocket, lit it, and took a drag. As he let the smoke drift slowly out of his mouth, he smiled. Sheriff Gordon had no plans that included anyone other than himself once the land was sold to the railroad. "What's three more graves in Boothill?" he said to himself as he got up, hitched up his belt, picked up his coffee, and headed for his office. "Those three are useful, but they're not very smart."

When they reached the bluff overlooking Twin Forks, Matt and the others turned off into the trees. They dismounted, rolled smokes, and stood in silence, looking at the town. Finally, Jacob snuffed his butt on the heel of his boot and said, "It won't get any easier standing here and looking at it. Let's get moving, Clay."

The two men mounted, and Clay turned to Matt. "You give us a good half hour before you start down. It'll take us that long to get to the creek without being seen from town. Then we should all get to town about the same time."

Matt nodded. "We've been over it enough times. Don't worry. You just see that Jacob doesn't fall off his horse. He's used to easy riding on wide trails."

Clay laughed, and Jacob just snorted. Both men turned their mounts into the trees and were soon lost from sight. Matt rolled another cigarette and sat down with his back against a tree. Drella rose from where she was sitting and crossed to Matt. She turned around three times and lay down beside him, her head across his boots. Matt reached down and scratched her rump, and Drella raised her head in ecstasy. "I know. Scratch your rump and you'll follow me anywhere." He moved his hand up and began to scratch behind her ears. "I don't know what to tell you, girl. I know I promised you no more fights, just a good life where you could chase rabbits and squirrels to your heart's content, and here I am again, about to enter the lion's den. But you like Maria—I know you do—and Culbertson's not such a bad guy. I promise you again that as soon as this business is over, I'll try to put my gun away." He looked at the dog. She was lying there with her eyes closed. Matt smiled. "I know you're just a dog, but I would rather keep my word to you than to most men I know." They sat like that a while longer, and then Matt got up, moved to Aphrodite, and tightened the cinch he had loosened earlier. "Well, ladies," he said to both animals, "I guess we had better be heading to meet whatever the gods have waiting for us." With that, he swung into the saddle and turned Aphrodite toward the trail that led to Twin Forks.

Sheriff Gordon saw Matt as he started down from the ridge that overlooked the town. He went to each man's hiding place and let them know that Matt was on his way into town and that he was coming in alone. He reminded them to wait until Matt was leaving his office. Then the sheriff returned to his office and put his feet up on his desk. He pulled out his pistol and checked the action. Before he put it back in the holster, he slipped a shell into the chamber that he normally kept empty.

Chapter Twenty-seven

Jacob and Clay had made their way across the creek and moved toward the outskirts of town. They had decided that the best plan of attack would be for each to enter the town from different ends, conceal themselves, and watch for the ambush they were certain would occur. As they parted, they gave each other a thumbs-up. Jacob moved to the west end and rode toward the center until he had a clear view of the sheriff's office. Then he reined in alongside a storage shed, dismounted, and took his rifle from the scabbard. Clay rode up to the back of the livery stable, tied off his horse, and climbed up into the hayloft. He moved to the front of the loft, where he knew he would have a clear view of the sheriff's office. There he settled down against a pile of hay with his rifle across his lap and waited.

Buster was sitting in a chair outside the general store, looking at a catalog he had borrowed from Paul Higgens. The pictures were his main interest, but he sometimes wished he had learned to read, particularly when he encountered something that he didn't understand. Currently he was trying to figure out what a three-legged stool was for.

Sam was up on the second floor of the Lucky Lady. He had the window open so he could step out on the veranda when the time came. He was sipping from a bottle of whiskey. What the hell did the sheriff know? He needed a sip or two to settle his nerves. Even though the bottle was now half empty, Sam knew it wasn't having any effect on him at all.

Curly was at the back of the alley across the street from Gordon's office. He was thinking about what Gordon had said this morning. He didn't trust the sheriff any farther than he could spit, but he needed him because Gordon had the money to buy the land at dirt-cheap prices. Curly was a patient man, though, and he could wait until the sheriff made his deal with the railroad people. Then he would make his move for a bigger share of the pie. Maybe even the whole pie.

As he rode into Twin Forks, Matt caught himself thinking how much he liked small sleepy towns. Nothing much, just the necessities, that was what appealed to him. There was little activity in the town, a couple of horses tied to the hitch rail at the Lucky Lady, a woman entering the general store, a man sitting in front of the store reading, and that was all. Drella had dropped back to walk alongside Aphrodite. She had learned very early that when entering a town, she was better off sticking close to Matt. Kids with stones and storekeepers with brooms frequently took exception to a dog who simply wanted to sniff the smells of new surroundings.

Matt turned in at the hitch rail in front of the sheriff's office. He hadn't noticed anything out of the ordinary on his way in, although he thought he had seen the man sitting in front of the general store before, but he couldn't place him for certain. In any case, he didn't relax his vigil, and he made a mental note to remember that a man was sitting in front of the general store. He tied Aphrodite off and started toward the door to the office. Drella turned around a couple of times and lay down under the front window of the sheriff's office as Matt went in.

Sam watched Matt ride in. Sam followed Matt with his eyes until Matt turned in to the hitch rail at the sheriff's office, where Sam lost sight of him. *How easy it would have been to drop the gunfighter as he rode by,* Sam thought, as he took another pull from the bottle. He waited a few seconds longer, and then he stepped through the window onto the balcony and moved to the end, where he had a clear view of the sheriff's office.

Across the street, Clay also watched as Matt rode up to the sheriff's office. He searched the area for any sign of movement that might indicate an ambush, but he saw nothing. He was about to relax after Matt entered the building, when he saw Sam step out onto the balcony across the street. Clay carefully and quietly levered a shell into his Winchester. He glanced back at the sheriff's office and saw Drella rise and then move across the street. "So, there are at least two," Clay muttered to himself as he turned his attention back to the balcony of the Lucky Lady.

Buster waited until Matt had gone inside before putting the catalog down and moving to stand next to a post, where he had a clear view of the front door to Gordon's office. Buster was thinking that he sure was glad they had decided to wait until Stoker came out of the office. He had noticed the gunfighter was looking directly at him as he rode in.

Jacob saw Matt ride up to the hitch rail and enter the office. He too had been watching for any signs of a trap and had seen nothing until Matt had gone in. Then he saw the man sitting in a chair outside the general store get up and move to a post at the end of the porch, where he stopped. "He has a clear view of the door where Matthew went in," Jacob said to himself as he took the hammer guard off his Colt. Then the marshal saw Drella get up and move across the street. "I hope you see her, Matthew. She's showing you where one of them is."

Curly saw Matt enter the sheriff's office. He moved a little closer to the end of the alley, but not so close that he could be seen. Curly's mind was on bigger things, and gunning down Stoker was just the beginning. He didn't pay any attention to the dog that crossed the street. He kept his eyes fastened on the door.

"Hello, Stoker. Come on in."

"I understand you want to ask me some questions, or are you simply going to lock me up?" Matt noticed the sheriff was wearing a vest that had a concho missing from it just like the one he found on the trail near Henry Johnson's body, and he realized that the stakes had just been raised. Not only was Gordon probably in on the land scheme, but it now appeared that he had been present when Henry Johnson was shot.

"I'm sorry about all the talk of you killing Johnson," Gordon said. "I was given bad information. I just want to know how you found the body and whether or not you had any idea who might have shot him."

Matt turned and moved to the window. As he related to the sheriff how he and Clay found the body, leaving out the finding of the concho, he watched Drella stand up. The hackles on the back of her neck were standing up, and she walked across the street and crouched down next to a storefront, watching the entrance to the alley. The shadows were such that Matt couldn't see very far into the alley, but he knew that Drella was watching with a purpose, which was good enough for him. When he had finished with his recollection of the events, he turned back to Gordon. "As to who did it, Sheriff, I don't know who in this town might be a back shooter, but given the goings-on since I've been here, you don't seem to have a shortage of them."

The smile faded from the sheriff's face, and his eyes hardened. He got up and stuck out his hand. "Well, thanks for coming in. Your reputation causes some folks to think the worst, I suppose. No hard feelings, I hope."

Matt took the hand and, fixing the sheriff with a hard, cold stare, said, "My reputation doesn't include back shooting and ambushing, and I think you know that." He dropped the hand. "However, I reserve hard feelings for people I respect." He turned toward the door, opened it, and turned back to see that the sheriff had started around the desk. "One other thing. I would imagine that Miss Johnson won't have any further problems or late-night visitors."

"Now that she and Culbertson are on good terms, I don't imagine she will," Gordon responded.

Matt felt the searing pain in his side a split second before he heard the shot. His gun was in his hand before the sound of the shot had died. He knew it had come from the alley, and he saw a blur of black fur moving toward the sound of the shot. Out of the corner of his eye, he saw the man from in front of the general store pointing a gun at him. Matt leaped from the boardwalk toward the hitch rail and snapped a shot at Buster. He didn't bother to watch the results but turned toward the alley. Drella had knocked Curly against the wall and then darted off. Matt fired just as Curly was lining up his second shot. At the same time, Matt heard gunfire to his right. He jerked his head in that direction in time to see a man fall from the second-story balcony of the Lucky Lady. Matt's attention returned to the man in the alley, when from behind he heard the sound of the hammer of a Colt being pulled back. He whirled and fired, but as he did, he heard the sound of another gunshot and knew that Gordon was dead before Matt's own bullet ever made contact. Matt surveyed the street. He saw Clay wave from the loft of the livery stable and knew what had happened to the fellow on the balcony. He looked in the other direction and saw Jacob walking toward him, leading his horse. He saw faces peering out windows and a few brave souls beginning to venture outdoors. He turned back toward the alley and saw Drella start toward him. He knelt down and waited for her. When she got to him, he put his arms around her and hugged her. "Thanks, big girl. I owe you one."

More people were coming outside. The storekeeper, Higgens, was one of the first to take everything in. He saw Jacob walking down the street. "Marshal, arrest this man! He just killed our sheriff."

"No, he didn't," Jacob replied. A crowd was beginning to gather, and there were grumblings of dismay and surprise at the marshal's words.

"What do you mean, he didn't?" Higgens asked. "Look around. It's as plain as the nose on your face. Who else could've done it?"

"I did," Jacob said. "He was about to shoot Matthew in the back. Why don't you get the town leaders together, and I'll explain everything." He moved over to Matt. "I saw you get hit. You'd better get it looked after. Clay, get him to a doctor or someone who functions as one. I'm going to meet with these people, and then I'll catch up with you at the Lucky Lady."

"Come on, Matthew. The barber serves as the medical authority for this place. Although after watching you work on Culbertson, you're probably better off taking care of yourself."

"Some things need to be handled by someone other than oneself, Clay," Matt said and then turned toward the marshal. "Jacob, you better send someone for the judge. He's the person to put all this in order, and we also need to discover if he was in on the whole thing or not."

"It's already on my list, but I've known him quite a while, and I don't think he was knowingly involved." Jacob watched Clay and Matt head toward the barbershop and then turned and walked toward the general store where Higgens was gathering people together.

Clay entered the barbershop with Matt trailing him. "Fred, this is Matthew Stoker. He got hit by a bullet a few minutes ago, and we were hoping you could take a look at it. Matthew, this is Fred Drummond."

Matt stepped forward and extended his hand. The barber shook it nervously, saying, "I'm not really a doctor, Mr. Stoker. People come to me with cuts and bruises, but I don't think I can handle anything serious."

"That's okay, Mr. Drummond. It's only a flesh wound. Do you have any antiseptic to clean it with?"

"I have some grain alcohol that I use on cuts. It burns like hell, but it does the job."

"That'll be fine," Matt said. "Have you ever sutured a wound?"

"Sutured? You mean sewed one up?" Matt nodded. "No, sir, I've never done that."

"Well, would you be willing to try if I supplied you with the necessities and told you what to do?"

"Sure, I suppose so. Will it take long? I'm a member of the town council, and they're having an emergency meeting over at Higgens' store."

"It'll only take a few minutes," Matt said and turned to Clay. "Would you go out to Aphrodite and get my saddlebags? And you might see if you can get a bottle of pain killer, or I might have to resort to Fred's grain alcohol."

Matt unbuttoned his shirt, took it off, moved to a straight-backed chair, and sat down. "Mr. Drummond, I don't see any point in waiting for Clay. Nothing in a bottle that really kills the pain. It simply makes a person not mind the pain so much."

Fred Drummond took the grain alcohol from the shelf, opened a drawer, and took out some gauze pads. He examined Matt's wound and then poured some alcohol on a pad and began to clean the wound. "You were right. It's only a flesh wound, but it's going to leave an ugly scar."

"That's why I want you to sew it up. Suturing not only keeps the wound clean and makes the healing quicker, but it cuts down greatly on the size of the scar."

"Well, this'll be a first for me, but if I can get the hang of it, I'll make some mothers happy. They're always bringing me their young 'uns when they've had an accident that opens a nasty gash."

"There's no great trick to it, and any medical house will have the thread and needles to do the job. Most people don't know it, but if you can sew a button on a shirt, you can suture a wound. The skin on the body is nothing more than wearing apparel, after all."

Clay came in just as Fred was finishing cleaning the wound. He handed Matt the saddlebags. Matt reached in and pulled out the cloth pouch. He opened it, looked down at the wound, and selected a needle and a spool of thread. "Looks like it will take twenty-five to thirty stitches," Matt said as he measured out a portion of thread and guided it through the needle's eye. He handed the needle to Fred and poured some alcohol over it, saying, "Just don't be afraid of using some force as you're piercing the skin. Try to keep the stitches as close together as possible and snug each one up tight before you go on to the next. There will be a little bleeding, but that's normal. After you're done, swab the entire area with alcohol. Clay, you should try to hold the wound together like we did with Culbertson. And where's that pain killer, anyway?"

Clay smiled and held out a bottle. "I asked for something that would help dull pain, and Hank gave me this."

"What is it?" Matt asked.

"Mescal. Hank said that a dentist gave him some when he was having a tooth pulled. He said he was pretty certain that he still felt some pain, but after two or three pulls of this stuff, he really didn't remember it hurting."

Matt brought the bottle to his lips and took a healthy pull. "All right, gentlemen. Let's get this over with."

The suturing, cleansing, and bandaging were handled in less than a half hour. When it was over, Matt asked Fred what he owed him for the work. Fred just shook his head as if to say that he wanted no payment, but Matt would have none of it. "Here's two dollars. When you use your skills to ease the pain and suffering of another, you should expect—even demand—to be rewarded. Otherwise people won't respect you or your work."

With that, he put on his shirt, turned, walked out the door, and headed with Clay to the Lucky Lady. Drella, who had been lying just outside the door, got up and followed. Fred locked the door of his shop and started toward the general store. When Clay and Matt entered the saloon, Hank saw them and asked how the mescal had worked.

Matt smiled and said, "You should portion that stuff out in small medicine bottles and sell it as a miracle cure. After anyone finishes a couple of swallows, they'll believe they're cured whether they are or not. Do you mind if my dog comes in with me?"

"No, as long as she doesn't bother my many customers."

The saloon was deserted. They ordered a couple of beers and moved to a table. Drella curled up under the table. Hank brought the beers and a bowl of water, which he put on the floor by Drella. "No reason she shouldn't have a drink too," he said.

"You have any problem with Clay drinking his in here?" Matt asked.

"No, sir, I don't, and as I understand it, the guy who made that rule won't object either."

"So what're you going to do now, Hank?" Clay asked. "Lock the place up until a new owner comes along?"

"Nah, I ran the place for Gordon. Did the ordering, kept the books, paid the help. I figure I'll keep the place going until everything's settled legally. I'm an honest man, which, if you don't mind my saying so, is rare in this town. I'll buy supplies, pay those who work, and take out my own wages. Then I'll put the rest in the bank in Kearney for whoever winds up owning the place. Afterward, I'll give the new owner a bill for my services. If he pays it, I'll stay. If not, I'll move on."

Two trail hands entered and moved to the bar. Hank went back behind the bar. "Howdy, gents. You new in town? The first drink's on the house. Everything after that requires cash. What'll you have?"

Matt and Clay finished their beers in silence and then ordered two more. After the next round arrived, Clay broke the silence. "I've been thinking about the offer you made the other day, and if it still goes, I'd like to take you up on it. I'm tired of moving from place to place. I'm ready to settle down, and I figure I'd have to go a long way before I got a better offer or found a better man to partner with."

"The offer still holds, and I'm glad you decided to accept. To tell you the truth, I was beginning to worry about having to handle the whole place by myself. I started identifying all the things that needed to be done to run a ranch successfully. The prospect was beginning to frighten me." Matt reached across the table, and he and Clay shook hands. "Welcome, partner."

Just then, Drella's tail began to thump against the floor. Matt smiled. "Jacob must be coming. When Drella decides on being someone's friend, it's always reflected through her tail. The damned thing can be lethal if you happen to be too close."

Jacob entered the saloon, waved to them, and stopped at the bar for a beer. He walked to the table, sat down, and took a long swig from the glass. "Trying to explain things to merchants and town fathers is thirsty work."

"How did it go?" Clay asked.

"I've had more receptive audiences," Jacob said. "First of all, when I told them what the sheriff was trying to do, they didn't believe me. Then Higgens piped up and told everyone that Gordon had been sending a number of documents to the county recorder. After that, they made me explain everything again. Then they wanted to know who was going to keep the peace in this town, which we all know is full of criminals committing violence. I don't think anyone has been put in that jail for anything more than drunk and disorderly in the entire history of this thriving community. But I explained to them that I was going to ask my superiors to assign a deputy marshal to this area. With the railroad coming through, there will be a need for a good lawman who doesn't choose sides. That seemed to make them feel a little better, but they were still worried about the notorious gunfighter who was currently in their town. I told them just to be sure to keep the women and children off the streets when you were around, Matthew."

"Thank you, kind sir. I don't know what I would do without you to enhance my reputation."

"It's the least I could do for a man who saved my life so that I could deal with the good people of this town. Anyway, I told them about what happened to Culbertson and how you doctored him, and the barber came in about then and said he could vouch for your medical skills. I also explained to them that a man frequently got a reputation more from gossip than fact. In general, I believe I put their minds at ease, and they needn't worry about you pillaging their town. I did tell them that you might go in for a little plunder." Jacob laughed at that and went for another beer. He was still chuckling when he returned to the table.

"Very funny," Matt said. "Did you send someone for the judge? I'd like to get this all straightened out before I leave."

"I'll take care of that myself. I should be able to get him here sometime tomorrow or the next day. How long are you planning to stay around?"

"Long enough to see the judge. I plan to head for Colorado afterward. I don't want to leave without presenting my take on the events that have occurred. There are enough fairy tales about my activities circulating without having these folks add to them."

Jacob nodded in agreement. "That's true enough. Why, I've heard some stories about you that would make women and children hide under the bed at the mere mention of your name. Of course, I spread most of them myself." Jacob smiled, pushed his chair back, and stood up. "Well, I'd best be heading for headquarters. I promised these folks a deputy, so I'd better see to it. I should be back before you leave. I'd like to say good-bye. I assume you'll be staying at the Johnson spread."

Matt nodded. "The food's good, and Drella likes Maria. By the way, Jacob, Clay has agreed to come in with me as a partner in the ranch."

"I'm really glad to hear that," Jacob said as he reached across and shook Clay's hand. "Congratulations, Clay, although teaming up with Matthew might be dangerous to your health. The man just can't seem to stay out of trouble."

"Funny how most of that trouble so often comes about when a certain U.S. marshal gets into something over his head." Matt chuckled.

"By golly, there's some truth in that, I'm sorry to say. Well, I had better get going." The marshal reached down and scratched Drella behind the ears. "See you later, old friend. Take care of these folks. They need all the help they can get. Matthew, Clay." Jacob tipped his hat to both and started out, but Matt stopped him.

"I think you better have this," Matt said as he reached into his vest pocket and took out the concho. "I found it next to Henry Johnson's body. I think you'll find it came from the vest the sheriff has on."

"I'll take a look right now. It would certainly remove all doubt." Jacob took the concho and left.

Matt and Clay finished their beers. Matt put some money on the table and, waving to Hank, the two left the Lucky Lady. They got their mounts and headed for the Johnson spread, with Drella leading the way. Faces at windows and heads stuck out of doorways watched them depart. "I don't reckon these folks are sorry to see us go," Clay said. Matt nodded in agreement and urged Aphrodite into a gentle lope.

Chapter Twenty-eight

They rode in silence until they were in sight of the ranch. "Buckboard in the front yard," Clay said. "They must be getting ready to take Mr. Culbertson back to the Circle C." As they rode on toward the ranch house, a voice called out, announcing their arrival. Bodies came out of the barn and the house. By the time they reached the house, a sizable crowd had formed.

"Thank God you've come back safely," Maria said as she knelt down to give Drella, who had rushed up to her, a big hug. "Where's Jacob? Is he all right?"

"Jacob is fine," Matt said. "He's gone to his main office. He should be back in two or three days."

Leaning on a cane for support, Culbertson said, "Tell us what happened. Was there any trouble?"

Matt and Clay recounted in general terms what had occurred in town, giving most of the credit to Jacob. They indicated that the judge would probably be in town within the next couple of days.

"Is it all right with you if we use your barn as our hotel for a couple of days?" Matt asked Maria.

"No problem," Maria said. "Mr. Culbertson has left a couple of hands to help Earl with the spring branding, and I asked one of them to bring a steer down from the meadow and dress it out, so we have plenty of food."

Clay dismounted and walked over to Earl. "You know, Earl, with all that Gordon and the others were into, I wouldn't be surprised that we haven't taken care of those responsible for the death of your father. It seems pretty clear to me that Gordon came here with a plan in mind that included his being sheriff. That way he could control most any situation that might arise."

"I think you could be right, Clay. In any case, I'm going to look at it that way and get on with my life, and it looks like Maria's going to be a big part of that life." A big smile crossed Earl's face.

"That's great," Clay said, shaking Earl's hand. "Congratulations."

"Nothing's definite yet, but I'm pretty sure it will be soon," Earl said.

Culbertson, after hearing about the judge, said that he would send a hand into town so that everyone would be informed when the judge arrived. He said it would allow him to give his will to the court itself and make everything legal. Then John Culbertson, helped by Billy, climbed into the buckboard. Billy signaled to the Circle C riders who were not staying to help with the branding, and they started off toward the Circle C.

Chapter Twenty-nine

Three days later, Matt and Clay were getting ready to leave. They tied their gear behind their saddles and led their horses toward the house. Matt noticed Drella stop and sniff the air. Then her tail slowly began to wag.

"Rider coming," Clay said.

"Look at Drella's tail. It must be Jacob," Matt said.

When they reached the house, the door opened, and Maria and Earl came out on the porch.

"Guess what?" Earl said.

"From the looks of both of you with those raccoon smiles on your faces," Matt said, "I would guess that Earl asked Maria to marry him, and she accepted. What do you think, Clay?"

"I don't think anything else could make people look that silly," Clay replied. "Still and all, it's about time. Earl has been mooing around like a calf that lost its mommy ever since we got here."

"You two think you're so smart," Maria said. "The truth is I asked him. If I had waited for him to pop the question, I'd be old and in my grave." Earl turned a deep shade of red and stared at his boots as she spoke. Then Matt called their attention to Jacob's approach. Maria said, "This is perfect. All of the people close to me are here for the news. You two can't leave now. You have to stay for the wedding."

"Besides that," Earl said, "Maria and I have been talking about how best to make this ranch a success. Clay, we'd like you to stay and help us run this place. You probably have more know-how about ranching than the two of us put together."

Clay took off his hat and started twisting it around in his hands. "Earl, Maria," he said, "that's one of the finest offers I've ever had, but Matthew has offered to make me his partner in the new ranch he's purchased, and I've accepted. Anyway, you won't have any problems here with Mr. Culbertson and Billy around to help."

"That's terrific, Clay," Maria said. "Now we have even more to celebrate. Your partnership with Matthew and mine with Earl. You two just have to stay."

Matt shook his head. "We'd really like to, Maria, but we've got a lot to do if we're going to start this new life. We'll definitely try to make it back for the wedding."

"Hello," Jacob said as he rode in. "Got the coffee on?"

"We do, indeed," Earl said. "And an apple pie just out of the oven made by my soon-to-be bride."

"Now, there's a big surprise. What took you so long to ask her?"

"He didn't. She asked him," Clay said. "Good to see you, Marshal."

"You don't say so. Maybe I made a mistake if this young fellow can't get around to asking important questions." Jacob looked at the two horses loaded with blankets and saddlebags. "Doesn't look like you were going to wait for me. You're not staying for the wedding?"

"We've already covered that, but you can fill in for us. You know that Maria will need someone to give her away. You're the only person here old enough to do that," Matt said.

"No," Earl chimed in. "Since you and Clay won't be available, I'll need Jacob to be my best man. Besides, Mr. Culbertson is the perfect person to give the bride away. We'll ask him."

Maria clapped her hands together and nodded in agreement. "That's perfect, Earl! He's already done so much for us. It would be wrong for us to leave him out of what's going to be the biggest moment of our lives," Maria said. "We'll ride over and ask him today. And, Jacob, don't you dare refuse to be Earl's best man."

Jacob dismounted and took off his hat. "I would be honored to serve as your best man," he said to Earl. "But Maria may not even want me at the wedding when she hears what I have to say. Earl, I'm here to offer you a position as deputy United States marshal. The pay is fifty dollars a month, a new horse of your choosing, and all the ammunition you need. The ranch here is nearly in the center of your assigned territory, so you can use it as your home base. What do you say?"

Surprisingly, Maria answered for him. "We had a long talk about this, and as a very wise person pointed out to me, the time has not yet come for good men to put away their guns. Earl will accept your offer, Jacob, and I'll spend sleepless nights worrying about him when he's not home. As he pointed out to me, it's who he is and what he does." She looked at Matt, and he smiled and touched his hat to her.

"All right," Jacob said. He had Earl raise his right hand and swear an oath, and then he pinned a badge on Earl's shirt. Earl seemed to stand a few inches taller. "Now let's go in and have some of that pie and coffee."

"Sorry," Matt said, "but we have to get going." He and Clay shook hands with Earl and gave Maria a hug.

"Well, hold on one minute," Jacob said as he walked back to his horse and reached into his saddlebag and pulled out a book. "I've been carrying this around for a few months and have been meaning to give it to you ever since I ran into you."

Matt took the book and opened it. "A first edition of *Madame Bovary.* Where did you find this?"

"It was on a shelf in a store in Wichita. I asked the storekeeper what it cost, and he told me that if I could read it to take it. I told him that I couldn't, but I had a friend who could, and he said to go ahead and take it because it wasn't worth anything to him."

"You know it's worth a great deal to me," Matt said. He reached out and took Jacob's hand. They shook, and then Matt pulled the marshal in and gave him a hug. "Take care, my friend."

"Next time we meet can't come soon enough," Jacob said. He stuck out his hand. "Clay, you're a good man.

Take care of this troublemaker." They shook and Clay nodded. Then Jacob dropped to one knee. "Drella, when you get tired of their lousy cooking, come and find me, and I'll fix you some tortillas and pony." The dog licked his face, and the marshal gave her a big hug.

Matt and Clay mounted. Matt turned to Earl and Maria and said, "The next time we visit, try not to offer us so much excitement."

"Wait a minute!" Maria cried, and she ran around the corner of the house. A minute later she came running back to Aphrodite and Matt. She reached up and handed him a red carnation. "For you, Sir Knight."

Matt took the flower and carefully threaded it through the uppermost buttonhole on his vest. Then he took off his hat and leaned down and gave Maria a kiss on the cheek. "Never has a knight received a token of greater worth from a fairer maiden."

Matt and Clay turned their mounts and started out, Drella leading the way. Suddenly, Matt turned back and looked at the three people standing on the porch. He took the sight in for several seconds, then touched his hat, turned Aphrodite, and rode off.